THE WORLD'S
WORST
Mothers

About the author

Sabine Ludwig was born in Berlin in 1954. After graduating, she worked as a radio editor. She is now one of Germany's most successful writers for children, and she also translates the books of authors such as Eva Ibbotson and Kate DiCamillo from English into German. She lives in Berlin with her husband and daughter.

About the translator

Siobhán Parkinson was born in Dublin in 1954. After graduating, she worked as a book editor. She is now one of Ireland's most successful writers for children and is Ireland's first Children's Laureate. She has translated books by Renate Ahrens and Burkhard Spinnen from German into English. She lives in Dublin with her husband.

THE WORLD'S WORST Mothers

SABINE LUDWIG

Translated by
Siobhán Parkinson

THE WORLD'S WORST MOTHERS
Published 2012
by Little Island
7 Kenilworth Park
Dublin 6W
Ireland

www.littleisland.ie

First published as *Die schrecklichsten Mütter der Welt* by Cecilie Dressler Verlag in Hamburg
in 2009

Copyright © Cecilie Dressler Verlag 2009
Translation copyright © Siobhán Parkinson 2012

The author has asserted her moral rights.

ISBN 978-1-908195-19-7

British Library Cataloguing Data. A CIP catalogue record for this book is
available from the British Library.

Cover design by Chris Judge
Inside design by www.sinedesign.net

Printed in Poland by Drukarnia Skleniarz.

Little Island received financial assistance from
The Arts Council (An Chomhairle Ealaíon), Dublin, Ireland.

The translation of this work was supported by a grant from the Goethe-Institut
which is funded by the German Ministry of Foreign Affairs.

The publisher acknowledges the financial assistance of Ireland Literature Exchange
(translation fund), Dublin, Ireland.
www.irelandliterature.com
info@irelandliterature.com

10 9 8 7 6 5 4 3 2 1

Chapter 1

Bruno lifted up the bag. It was dead heavy, but still way too light for training.

His boxing gloves were lying on the lawn beside the path that led from the patio into the garden. Bruno's father had had it re-sanded the week before. He would put on the gloves in a minute, but first he had to fill this stupid bag.

Bruno was holding the bag open with one hand, and with the other he was trying to stuff it with a shovelful of sand. It was not easy. It had rained yesterday, and the sand was way too wet. And now he'd got it all over his shoes.

You could always buy a punchbag, of course. They didn't cost much. But it wasn't a question of money. It was a question of his mother.

He had been allowed to keep the boxing gloves that his father gave him for Christmas, 'but only for show', he'd had to promise.

'They look class on my wall.'

'I don't think they really fit in,' his mother had replied.

And Bruno had to admit she was right. His boxing gloves didn't look quite right under the poster of Mozart as a child in a blue satin suit with a lacy flounce at the throat.

'You're not planning to use them, I take it?' His mother had sounded anxious.

His father rolled his eyes and said, 'Well, since you have refused to let him have a punchbag, what could he possibly *use* them for?'

'Think of his fingers!'

Bruno thought about his fingers, which, at the moment, looked like battered sausages. His precious fingers, which nothing could be allowed to harm, because that would be the end of his piano playing, the end of his career as a pianist.

He was getting there. One more shovelful and he would be able to tie the bag at the top and hang it from a branch of the oak tree.

'Bruno!' The sound echoed through the garden.

The shovel slipped, and a load of wet sand landed in Bruno's sleeve.

'It's time to go to piano! Get a move on!'

Bruno shook out his sleeve and looked at his watch. Five past four. He'd forgotten all about his piano lesson. He'd been forgetting about it more and more often lately, even though it was a date written in stone. For the past year, he'd had to turn up every Thursday at a quarter past four at Frau Leberknecht's in Leonore Street.

He brushed his hands down quickly on his trousers. What about the bag? Where should he hide it? He stuck it behind the box hedge, a place his mother would never dream of looking.

Bruno lurched through the patio door into the house, grabbed his music, which was lying on the piano, and stuffed it into his shoulder bag. Only seven minutes left. He'd just make it, if he really put the boot down. Frau Leberknecht hated it when people were late.

'Are your hands clean?' Bruno's mother's head appeared around the kitchen door.

'Yeah, sure,' he lied. He didn't have time for hand-washing.

Bruno threw his bag over his shoulder, leapt onto his bike and sped off. Too late, he remembered that he'd left his boxing gloves lying in the garden. *Please, don't let it rain!*

It was exactly eighteen minutes past four when he rang Frau Leberknecht's doorbell. He wiped his hands once more on his trousers.

Frau Leberknecht opened the door, said, 'Good afternoon, Bruno,' and went ahead of him into the room with the grand piano. The first time Bruno's mother had seen that grand piano, she was bowled over. It was enormous and its black lacquered wood was always gleaming as if it had just been polished. It seemed to say to Bruno, 'You're not good enough for me. You will never be good enough for me.'

Bruno feared nothing the way he feared this monster.

Frau Leberknecht opened the lid and Bruno pulled the music out of his bag and put it on the stand.

'We'll start with the Chopin,' said Frau Leberknecht. 'You were having a few problems with that the last time, weren't you?'

He always had problems with the Chopin. Four sharps and then that impossible stretch with the left hand.

'Begin.'

The fingers of his right hand, which should have been gliding smoothly over the keys, felt as if they had got themselves into a knot. His left hand was hanging uselessly in the air. From low G to high C – how could he do that?

'What key are we in here?' asked Frau Leberknecht as if she

couldn't care less, but Bruno could see that deep down she was peppering. Every mistake you made, she took it personally. Even the piano let out an uncooperative groan, as Bruno pressed the pedal.

'E major,' whispered Bruno.

'Well then, please play it in E major,' said Frau Leberknecht.

Bruno began to sweat. His fingers were slippery. And what was all this? Why had the white keys suddenly turned brown? It took him a moment to work out that it was his own sweat mixed with sand from the punchbag. Hastily he tried to wipe the dirt off the keys with his fingers, which led to a horrible noise.

'Please go and wash your hands,' said Frau Leberknecht as his index finger slithered off a streaky C key.

Cheeks flaming, Bruno stood up and went to the door. Then he hesitated. He didn't know where the toilet was. The only bit of Frau Leberknecht's flat that he knew was this room – that and the hallway.

'On the right by the front door,' said the teacher.

He could see his blazing face in the mirror. A little brown trickle ran down his forehead to his nose, heading for his mouth. He licked it away. It tasted of salt and sand.

❄

'Look, Sofa, look what I've made!' Nicholas came stumbling into Sophie's room. He was carrying a semi-collapsed mini-sandcastle in both hands.

'Don't!' shouted Sophie. But it was too late. Nicholas dropped the heap of sand on her desk. She just managed to get her laptop closed before a shower of sand landed on it.

4

'Are you crazy?' she yelled.

Sophie sighed when her mother appeared a moment later.

'Really, Sophie! Why do you always have to shout at Nicholas like that?'

Sophie pointed at the heap of sand on her desk.

'Oh, for goodness' sake, a little bit of sand is easily got rid of.'

'Have you any idea what would have happened if it had got into my computer?' Sophie couldn't help the way her voice was getting shriller and shriller. 'That would have been the end of it, and you'd have had to buy me a new one.'

'Might be just as well if the wretched thing finally gave up the ghost. Then you might do something other than hunching over it day and night.'

'Oh, yeah? And what would you suggest?'

'You could start by combing your hair, for example. You look like a scarecrow.'

Sophie's mother's haircut was short and precise. Not a hair out of place.

'And another thing you could do for a change would be to play with your little brother instead of nagging him all the time.'

'Maybe if he could learn my name ...' Sophie turned away. She didn't want her mother to see that the tears were starting in her eyes.

'Oh, don't be so sensitive. Everyone else thinks it's cute. But you have to make such a fuss about it.'

Her mother left the room, shaking her head. She came back with a dustpan and brush.

'I'll do it,' said Sophie quickly.

Nicholas had poured the sand right onto her maths test, and she didn't want her mother to see that it was not great. She'd much rather get George to sign it. He wasn't really supposed to, as he wasn't her guardian, just her mother's husband, but the maths teacher didn't know that, did he?

Sophie opened the window to throw the sand out into the yard. Nicholas was down there, hunkering happily in the sandpit, filling bucket after bucket with sand. She dropped the sand right onto his head and then quickly closed the window so that she wouldn't have to listen to the racket he made.

Then she opened her laptop and cleaned a few grains of sand off the keys. She logged into Allfriends. It worked. She breathed a sigh of relief. And there was a new post. Someone called Leonie asked if she was the Chiara who'd been in fifth class with her. She couldn't be sure from the photo.

Of course she couldn't. Nobody could recognise Sophie from that photo. She had combed her long hair in front of her face and taken her own picture with her mobile phone.

And anyway she wasn't called Chiara and she hadn't ever been in fifth class in Lilienthal Grammar. Only really good students attended Lilienthal Grammar. Sophie was not a good student. Nor was she fifteen. She was thirteen. But every time she went online as pretty, sporty Chiara, whose hobbies were playing tennis and the saxophone, she forgot all about the real Sophie, the chubby girl with pimples on her forehead and chewed nails who had never as much as held a tennis racquet in her hand, never mind a saxophone. Of course Chiara had no brothers or sisters, and definitely no half-brother with blond curls and sky-blue eyes that everyone thought was a little angel.

A soft mewing could be heard.

'Come here, Lulu, come on.'

The cat turned onto its back in front of Sophie and let her give her a thoroughly good scratching. Lulu was the only one in the whole family who was not taken in by Nicholas. She'd actually bitten him once, when he was trying to pull her out from under a cupboard by the tail.

'We're two poor little sausages, aren't we?' said Sophie.

Lulu meowed something that sounded to Sophie like, 'Yes, that's right.'

❄

'Emily, have you seen the car keys?'

Emily looked up from her English book. She only had ten minutes left and she had to learn two pages of vocabulary. She'd never make it.

'Are they not in the box?' she asked.

'No, or I wouldn't have asked, would I?'

Half hysterical, one arm stuck into her coat sleeve, Emily's mother was barging through the kitchen. She yanked out the cutlery drawer, snatched a newspaper off the table.

'I was sure I'd left them here on the table!'

Emily shut her book.

'Why do you put the keys in a different place every time, Mum?'

'Because … because the phone was ringing as I came in yesterday …'

Emily got up and went to the little cupboard in the hallway on which the phone sat. There were the car keys, under the telephone book. She swung them triumphantly from her fingers.

'Here they are, Mum.'

'Thanks, Emmykins! What would I do without you?'

Emily wondered the same thing. Every day. Actually, she thought she'd already solved the problem of the keys. She'd given her mother a present of an electronic key fob that beeped if you whistled for it. Or so the leaflet said. The thing was, though, that her mother couldn't whistle. But that didn't stop the wretched thing from beeping incessantly.

It started up once when her mother was doing a job interview. She'd rooted about frantically in her handbag without finding the keys, but the contents of her bag tumbled out onto the floor. Including Porky, a lucky piggy that Emily had made for her in first class. It only had one ear and didn't look too appetising. Of course she didn't get the job. Who would employ a book-keeper who wasn't able to keep her own handbag under control?

'Do you want a lift? It's raining. You'll have to sit in the back,' her mother said as they reached the little yellow Fiat dotted with rusty flecks, for all the world like freckles. 'The passenger door is stuck.'

'It's been stuck for months,' said Emily. 'Why don't you get it fixed?'

Her mother laughed and said, 'I will if I get this job today. I have a really good feeling about this one.'

She had a really good feeling about them all. But she never got the job. She was too old, or the boss didn't like her being a single mother who didn't want to do overtime. Once, she'd even turned a job down because the woman she would have to share an office with used a perfume that was too overpowering. 'I couldn't put up with that stink for two minutes,' she'd said.

'Oh my God!' Emily's mother was tapping on the petrol gauge. 'Either this is wonky again or we're in trouble.'

They were in trouble. The car chose the middle of a junction to grind to a halt.

Emily leapt out of the car and flew to the bus stop. A bus was just coming. Whew! As it drew up, she caught sight of her mother in the middle of the junction, surrounded by honking drivers and swinging an empty petrol can.

She wasn't going to get this job either.

Chapter 2

While Emily's mother was standing at a busy junction in the middle of Berlin, desperately looking for a kind-hearted motorist who might let her have a little petrol, a man entered a factory a few hundred kilometres further north.

He hurried past shelves that were stuffed with cardboard boxes. On the front of every box was a diagram of what was in it. Dolls, soft toys, cranes, fire engines. Toys, in other words. But not ordinary toys. The toys from Wohlfarth's toy factory were technical masterpieces. There were dolls that could not only speak but also cry real tears. Dogs that lay on their backs to have their tummies scratched and even did real poops, only ones that didn't smell. Aeroplanes that not only could fly but landed on the exact spot that you'd programmed them to land on.

Walther Wohlfarth, the founder of Wohlfarth's Toys, had made a fortune out of his crying dolls and his lifelike dogs and cats, but then the whole business went rapidly downhill because people started buying their toys from the Far East, where they could make toys that were at least as smart and looked almost exactly the same but sold at only half the price.

It was Walther Wohlfarth himself who was striding past the remains of his once thriving business without as much as a glance at all the Bellos, Fluffies, Tinas and Ginas who stared out of lifeless glass eyes.

'Kruschke!' he yelled. 'Kruschke, where the blazes are you?'

'Here, boss,' came a muffled voice from behind a shelf. 'I'm just coming.'

A fat little man with a bald patch appeared. He looked fairly stressed. His braces were hanging down and his shirt had been buttoned up wrongly. There were beads of perspiration on his forehead. His left eye was twitching and his right eye was staring straight ahead. He was not what you'd call a good-looking man.

'She got away, boss,' he blurted out. 'Prototype 3131. Just took off.'

'Kruschke!' thundered Wohlfarth. 'You are an idiot!'

Kruschke shrank back.

'Yes, boss.'

Kruschke, however, was far from an idiot. The complicated technical inner workings of all the toys around him were his sole work. No one would have guessed that this red-faced little man with a squint was one of Germany's most important inventors.

'You are an idiot, Kruschke,' Wohlfarth said again. 'I told you to reprogram her. How could this have happened?'

'Just as I was about to install deep-sleep mode she upped and left.' Kruschke chanced a little laugh as he added, kind of proudly, 'She's pretty smart.'

'Smart! *Smart!*' hissed Wohlfarth. 'You made a mess of her. Get her back and then shred her.'

'You want me to … *murder* her?' stammered Kruschke.

'We don't need Prototype 3131 any more. We'll write her off as a mistake. Just you find her, and make it snappy!'

11

'Yessir. On my way, boss!'

Kruschke ran as fast as his stubby little legs would carry him out of the factory.

'I'd get rid of that fellow in a flash,' murmured Wohlfarth, 'if only I didn't need him so badly.'

He plucked a piece of fluff off his sleeve before he also left the factory floor.

✿

Kruschke was standing on a dune, the wind ruffling the few strands of hair that he had left.

'Sarah!' he called. 'Sarah!'

If she was within a hundred metres, she'd have to hear him and react to him. That was how he'd programmed her.

Sarah was a nice name. That was what the girl who'd sat in front of him in first class had been called. She'd had thick chestnut-brown hair. He couldn't take his eyes off it. When the sun shone through the classroom window, Sarah's hair gleamed reddish gold. He'd tried to find hair in that same colour for *his* Sarah.

Wohlfarth, of course, said that a prototype didn't need hair, that it was a waste of money, but Kruschke had insisted. 'That's the only way we can tell if she's convincing. Hair is very important.'

But then Wohlfarth had decided on blonde hair for the next ones. 'Blonde is just nicer, more trustworthy. Scientific studies have proved that.'

Wohlfarth was right. He was always right. Well, he was the boss. But for how long?

Kruschke ran down the dune to the beach.

'Sarah!' he called again.

But the beach was empty. Seagulls were screeching. There was a smell of rotten seaweed. It wasn't easy to hide, here on the island. He'd have to find her before her batteries ran out. He had to explain to her what he had in mind for her. He knew she'd understand that she was meant for great things: to be the world's most perfect woman.

She was beautiful and clever, but she was missing something vital. And he, Kruschke, could give her that very thing. Nobody else – only he could do it!

But where *was* she?

A woman walked out of the dunes. Her long brown hair streamed in the wind. Although it was noticeably cool on this April morning, she was wearing only a thin summer dress. She marched quickly over the sand to the water's edge. She kept going till the foam washed over her bare feet. She raised her arms as if to embrace the horizon.

Kruschke had opened his mouth to call her name, but he said nothing. He might startle her and she'd be off again. He couldn't follow her any further, and anyway he was out of breath.

He struggled through the sand to her.

'Sarah,' he said softly. 'Sarah, stand still. Don't go into the water, do you hear me?'

Sarah turned around to face him.

'Water is a chemical combination of the elements hydrogen and oxygen. You can drink water. You can bathe in water,' she said with a smile.

'That's right,' said Kruschke. 'But you can't bathe in *this* water, Sarah.'

'Bathing is fun,' said Sarah and walked on.

✳

An hour later there was a knock on Wohlfarth's office door. His office was a gallery in the former finishing room of the factory, and you could look down through a large glass window at the assembly line where, many years previously, the workers had fixed the dolls' hair and dressed them before they were packed into boxes

Wohlfarth was sitting at a computer, staring at the screen.

The knock came again.

'Come in, Kruschke.'

Kruschke opened the door carefully and slithered through the crack.

'Excuse me, boss … but …' he stuttered.

'Don't tell me she's escaped!' Wohlfarth was getting red in the face.

'Unfortunately, she has. I nearly had her, but then she just threw herself into the sea. She said she wanted to bathe, and the next thing, there she was in the water.'

'Is Prototype 3131 salt-waterproof?'

'No. Her body can only tolerate fresh water between 19 and 38 degrees.'

Wohlfarth typed something into his computer.

'It's 15 degrees in the North Sea right now. How long do you think she'll last?'

Kruschke swallowed. 'Less than a day, I'm afraid.'

'Good. Let's just hope she won't land up here again some day.'

'Why?' asked Kruschke, confused.

'Because I don't want anyone on the island to hear of her

existence, that's why!' Wohlfarth stood up. 'And now, would you kindly get back to work. But I'm warning you: one more mistake like that and – '

'Don't worry, boss, it will never happen again,' said Kruschke quickly. 'In future, everything will go like clockwork.'

'I very much hope so. Never forget how much is depending on this!'

Chapter 3

When Bruno got home at lunchtime, he got a surprise.

'I have to talk to you,' said his mother, before he had time even to take his jacket off. 'I've been talking to Frau Leberknecht.'

'Oh, right?' said Bruno nervously. Had she made a complaint about how he'd mucked up the keys of her precious piano?

'I've given her notice.'

Bruno had to sit down. 'Great – I mean … why?'

'Because I don't think she's good enough for you. She just doesn't see the great talent she has right under her nose.'

Bruno sighed. The idea that his mother had finally twigged that he would never be a great pianist – it was too much to hope for. There was just going to be a new teacher, that was all. This had happened very often in the last few years. It was pretty miraculous that Leberknecht had lasted as long as she had.

His mother was pacing up and down. Even her back was furious.

'When I asked her if she had entered you in the piano competition in June, she went so far as to laugh! Apparently you're not good enough and it wouldn't be very nice for you to come last.'

Bruno sighed again, louder this time. His mother drove him nuts.

'But don't worry, darling. The woman just hasn't a clue. I never liked her. It was just that she came so highly recommended.'

Bruno remembered how delighted with Frau Leberknecht his mother had been at first.

'She's right for you,' she'd said. 'Not like that wimp Herr Karl with his wet-fish handshake. She'll bring you up to concert standard, I'm sure of it!'

She'd sung the praises of Herr Karl too, in the beginning, but later she blamed him for the fact that Bruno still didn't play like Clang Clang, the famous Chinese pianist she revered. She'd given Bruno his autograph with a personal message as a birthday present. He'd have preferred an autograph of Muhammad Ali any day.

Bruno's mother put a plate in front of him. 'I'm sorry I didn't get around to cooking anything today.' She opened the fridge and took out cheese and salami. 'I spent the whole morning ringing around.'

She put a slice of bread on Bruno's plate and beamed at him. 'But I've found the best one. The very best. Professor Griebel. It was very difficult because he doesn't really have any free slots, but when I told him that playing the piano is your great passion, that you can hardly wait to do your stuff on a great stage –'

'Mum!' Bruno tried to interrupt.

'Of course, he's much more expensive than Leberknecht, but it's worth it. It has to be worth it for the sake of your –'

'Mum!' said Bruno more loudly. 'I can't play the piano.' He pushed the plate away. He'd lost his appetite. 'Do you remember the first recital we had at Frau Leberknecht's? The girl who went before me?'

'The little Chinese girl?'

'Korean. Boy, could she play! And she was only seven. Now, *she* is talented. That's what Frau Leberknecht thinks too.'

His mother waved dismissively.

'That's Asians for you. They work ridiculously hard. You'll find she practises for six hours a day.'

'Mum! Your Clang Clang is Asian too,' Bruno said.

'He's completely different – a genius. But this girl … she had no soul, Bruno. It's all about soul. You were just too nervous that day; you weren't used to having an audience – that's why you played badly.'

'I play badly at home too. I don't need an audience to do it. I'm just no good!'

Bruno's mother took his hands and kissed them. A tear fell on the back of one of his hands. 'Don't say that. I know that's not true. I know I'm right. I'm your mother, after all.'

❀

I really have the worst mother in the world, Sophie typed into her computer.

She was in a chat room with a boy who called himself Dragon Monster. His photo showed a pale boy with hair gelled up who tried hard to look menacing. He was supposed to be sixteen. Sophie could see that this lad was fourteen, tops. But she was so furious with her mother that she'd have complained to a model in a shop window.

And the worst brother. Not that he's even my real brother. He collects dead animals. What a weirdo!

She was so annoyed, she totally forgot that she'd described herself as an only child in her profile. She scratched her forehead. Rats – another bloody pimple.

And my stepfather is the ... Sophie stopped. *The worst,* she was going to write, but that wasn't fair. George was actually very nice. At least he didn't always take Nicholas's side. But that could just be because he was fed up with the constant squabbling.

Sophie deleted the last few words and wrote: *And my stepfather hardly ever takes any notice of anything.*

So what does the old man do? wrote Dragon Monster.

He's a sales rep, answered Sophie.

Ugh! A door-to-door salesman? Revolting.

You said it.

But that didn't sound right either. George was a rep, but not the kind that goes from door to door. He worked for a pharmaceutical company that produced remedies for constipation and baldness, and his job was to inform doctors about new medication. He was always travelling. Sometimes he brought her back something really nice from Paris or the Maldives or wherever. She had a whole collection of T-shirts from all over the world. The one from Stockholm with the moose on it was her favourite.

Hey, are you still there? Dragon Monster wrote.

'Sophie! Are you coming? Dinner is ready,' called her mother from the kitchen.

'What are we having?' Sophie shouted back.

'Fish fingers with rice and salad.'

Sophie stuck her fingers down her throat. 'Puke, yuck,' she said under her breath.

Have to go and shovel some kind of muck into myself. Talk later, she typed.

I'll mail you something you might find interesting, came the reply. *Something funny.*

Sophie shook her head and turned the computer off. She knew all about Dragon Monster's idea of a joke. It was always some kind of questionnaire that told you if you were a green alien or were addicted to biros or were just plain mad. Sometimes they were a bit of fun, but mostly they were just stupid

She went into the kitchen and sat at the table. The whole flat stank of fried fish – again. If Nicholas had his way, they'd eat nothing else. Why couldn't he have a passion for chips or pizza?

Sophie pushed her fish fingers around in disgust and then gave a screech.

'What's wrong now?' asked her mother crossly.

'It was Nicholas!' yelled Sophie, pointing at a fat, half-squashed fly that had been lying under one of the fish fingers. 'Again! Remember the dead mouse he left on my bed?'

Sophie's mother took her plate and threw what was on it into the bin.

'Nonsense! The fly came from the salad, for sure, and as for the mouse, that was Lulu.'

'I wasn't even allowed to keep it,' said Nicholas.

Sophie's mother gave her a new plate.

'Will you please stop blaming Nicholas for everything.'

He nodded in agreement. 'I didn't do anything.'

'I know, my angel. Another couple of fish fingers? These ones here are nice and crispy.'

Nicholas already had a mountain of fish fingers on his plate and was chewing with his mouth open.

'Close your mouth. It's most unappetising,' said Sophie, taking a spoon of rice and two lettuce leaves.

'*You're* most unappetising,' said Nicholas, grinning cheekily.

'Did you hear that, Mum?' cried Sophie. 'Did you hear what he said?'

Her mother ruffled Nicholas's hair. 'Do you know what unappetising means, Nicky?'

'It means you are not hungry,' said Nicholas, looking at his mother as if butter wouldn't melt in his mouth. 'And Sofa isn't hungry, right?'

'See?' said his mother. 'He has no idea what it means.'

Sophie was convinced that Nicholas knew perfectly well. He was appalling, but he was smart. And she knew by the way he looked at her with his head on one side, letting half-chewed fish fall out of his mouth, that she was right.

✺

Emily looked at the clock. Where the hell was her mother? She was supposed to have just slipped out to buy milk and butter. That didn't take an hour. Maybe she'd had to take shelter somewhere. It was pouring rain and, as usual, she had no umbrella with her. But suppose something had happened to her?

Emily nearly fainted when the phone rang, but then she breathed a sigh of relief when she saw that the display identified Dad as the caller.

'Hello, chicken, how are you?' her father asked.

'Fine,' said Emily, trying to sound as cheery as possible. 'I got a B in maths!'

'You're joking! Really?'

'I came second in the class!'

'So all that work we did paid off.'

'Absolutely! Next week we have an English test. We can do a bit of work on that at the weekend.'

'Oh, what a pity! We were planning to go cycling at the weekend, and I was hoping you might come along.'

We were planning to go cycling! That 'we' made Emily sick. That was all she needed – to go cycling all over the countryside with her father and his girlfriend. It would look as if they were a family.

'I really don't have the time,' she said quickly. 'We have a biology test too.'

'Can you manage all that on your own?'

'No problem, there's always Mum.'

'And how is she?' her father asked. He asked that every time he rang, and every time Emily lied.

'Great.' And before he could ask if she'd finally found a job, Emily added, 'There's a ring at the door. She's probably forgotten her keys again.'

'Typical,' said her father with a laugh.

Emily put the phone down. Her parents had separated two years before. Emily had never asked why. She knew anyway. Her father had fallen in love with a woman who was totally different from her mother. A woman who did not suddenly remember two minutes before departure that she had left the tickets at home or that the iron was still turned on.

'You should be glad,' Emily's friend Charlotte had said. 'There's never a dull moment with your mother. Crazy things never happen to mine.'

The phone was ringing again. A mobile number that Emily didn't recognise.

'Hello?' she said tentatively.

'Emmykins!' came her mother's excited voice. 'Is my purse on the little cupboard in the hall?'

'No, Mum, there's nothing there.'

'Oh, God, then it must have been stolen. What on earth shall I do?'

'Where are you?' Emily could hear voices in the background. Angry voices, it seemed to her.

'Here in the supermarket. I just noticed at the checkout that my purse was gone. And I don't have my mobile either and –'

'Well, just leave the things there,' said Emily.

'Can't do that. I –'

Her mother's voice broke off and now some man was shouting in Emily's ear.

'Your mother has eaten an apple. An apple that she did not pay for. That's theft! Please come at once and bring the money. And you'll have to pay for the phone call too. Otherwise, I'll call the police!'

Emily hung up with a sigh. She went to get some money from her room. Then she pulled her jacket out of the wardrobe, grabbed an umbrella and set off to rescue her mother – again.

Chapter 4

The wind was whistling particularly strongly this morning around the old factory. An iron door was banging open and shut. The once white walls on the exposed side of the building were green with moss. Clumps of grass flourished on the roof, and there was even a little birch tree sprouting up between the roof tiles. It was being shaken back and forth in the wind.

The island where Wohlfarth's toy factory was situated was called Nordfall. It was just about an hour by boat from the mainland.

Over a hundred years ago, Nordfall had been twice as big as it was now. Wind and sea had gradually carried off more and more of the island, which lay like an elongated egg in the middle of the North Sea. At the broad end was the ferry port, next to a little collection of houses in which not much more than a dozen people were still living. They were mostly sheep farmers. Their sheep were pastured on the salt meadow behind the dyke.

The narrow end of the island was separated from the rest by a barbed-wire fence as tall as a man, which was higher on one side than the dyke and which ran along by the dunes on the other side as far as the sea.

The fence dated back to the time when Walther Wohlfarth's

toy factory had belonged to his father. Walther Wohlfarth Senior, however, had not been a maker of toys. He was much more interested in manufacturing hand grenades, cartridges, landmines and gunpowder. Wohlfarth's munitions factory had been in the family for generations before Walther Wohlfarth Junior broke with this tradition and started making dolls and teddy bears. But with competition from cheaply made toys from the Far East, Wohlfarth's toys had stopped selling, and eventually he had had to shut down his factory and let his employees go.

Kruschke had stayed on, though. He would not be parted from his creations. He went through the warehouse every day to check that they were all still working. He made Bella, a ballerina in pink, do a pirouette on the dusty floor, or he got The Amazing Somersaulting Poodle to do exactly five somersaults one after another before standing upright again on all four paws and giving a joyful woof.

Apart from Kruschke, three of the other former employees remained on Nordfall. Partly because they didn't know where else to go, and partly because they hoped that one day there might be work for them again.

That day had now arrived. Wohlfarth had asked them to come to his office at three o'clock on the dot. Two women and a man expectantly entered the factory. Vibke Paulsen led the way, a kindly and cheerful person who used to be in charge of the women who did the sewing. She made sure the hairstyles were all in order and that the little dolly clothes had no crooked seams. She was a native of Nordfall, the same as her husband, who rented out beach chairs in the summer.

Ramona Bottle came behind her. She used to be Wohlfarth's secretary. She was a bony blonde with long, pearly fingernails, which she filed and polished every day, as if she was just waiting for the moment when Wohlfarth would call on her to take dictation. She was very excited.

'Do you think the factory is going to open again?' she asked Vibke Paulsen.

'Hardly, with just the three of us,' answered Frau Paulsen. 'And anyway, bankrupt is bankrupt.'

'But I've heard it said that Kruschke has developed a totally new doll, an enormous one.'

'Yes. Apparently she ran half-naked over the dunes,' chipped in a wiry young man called Sven-Ole, who had been one of Wohlfarth's drivers. Nowadays he transported sheep from the island to the mainland. 'Hinnerk saw it himself.'

'What rubbish! Your cousin needs a new pair of glasses,' said Vibke Paulsen, laughing. 'I bet he believes in ghosts too!'

'Maybe Kruschke really has invented something new,' said Ramona Bottle hopefully. 'Something that might make real money.'

'Can an old fellow with a bald head get a lucky streak?' asked Sven-Ole, laughing at his little joke. 'Do you get it? Like streaks in your hair!'

'Oh, you and your silly nonsense,' said Vibke Paulsen, wagging her finger playfully at him.

The gate to the factory was opened. Kruschke waved them in.

'Hurry up. The boss is waiting.'

'It's such a shame, isn't it?' Vibke Paulsen whispered to Ramona Bottle, who was just stepping over a heap of something filthy, her nose wrinkling. 'The way it's all gone downhill.'

'Well, I just hope he isn't expecting us to clean this place up,' Ramona Bottle whispered back.

Wohlfarth was standing at the internal window, looking down at his ex-employees. Kruschke, fussing as usual, had already reached the stairs. Vibke Paulsen hadn't got any slimmer over the last few years, and Ramona Bottle hadn't got any younger. The only one who didn't seem to have changed was Sven-Ole. But then he was far too inexperienced to be of any real use.

Well, he'd just have to make the best of it. He had no choice and, more to the point, no money. He'd sunk every penny he had into this enterprise. If it went wrong, he'd be ruined for good.

He put his shoulders back. Why should it go wrong? The idea was simply stunning, and this time nobody was going to steal it. that was for sure.

He went behind his desk and straightened the big picture that hung on his wall.

'You will be proud of me, Mother,' he said. 'Very proud, even.'

At that moment, there was a knock on the door.

'Come in,' called Wohlfarth.

He's hardly changed, thought Ramona Bottle, looking at her former boss. *A few more grey hairs, maybe, and he looks a bit tired.*

'Good afternoon,' said Wohlfarth. 'Thank you for coming.' He smiled crookedly. 'Do sit down.'

He pointed at a couple of armchairs that were grouped with a sofa around a table. In the old days, only Wohlfarth's business partners were allowed to sit here. His former underlings sat carefully now on the sagging armchairs with their worn covers.

'I hope you all remember my ... our firm's motto.'

'Of course we do, boss,' said Sven-Ole. 'Something like

"If your child is happy, so is the world", or some such.' He stopped.

Ramona Bottle's hand flew up. '"Make your child happy and you save the world,"' she said proudly.

Wohlfarth nodded at her. 'That's right. That was exactly my slogan. More than that – it's the principle on which I have based my whole life. I, whose mother, God rest her soul' He made a pained face and pointed at the portrait behind him, which showed a kindly smiling lady with grey hair and a chain around her neck, on which hung a gold medallion. 'I who have my mother to thank for the happiest childhood that a man could possibly have, I've only ever wanted one thing: to make children happy. Because only happy children grow up into happy adults who can give something to the world, who can creatively engage …'

Sven-Ole wasn't listening any more. Why did the boss not just say straight out what on earth it was that he wanted from them? There wasn't even anything to drink on the table and not as much as a few dry biscuits to eat. He squinted at his watch and got a disapproving look from Ramona Bottle. Yeah, well, every word that dropped from Wohlfarth's lips was music to her ears. Everyone in the factory used to laugh at her. It really was funny how moonstruck she'd been. And she was supposed to be engaged at the time. Her fiancé had broken it off because all she did was waffle on about Wohlfarth. And here she was again, gazing at him as if she were a sheep and he a nice juicy bunch of grass. *Baa, baa.*

A new joke occurred to him: if a shepherd beats his sheep, does that make him a *baaaad* person? He had to bite his lip to prevent himself from laughing out loud.

Even Vibke Paulsen found it hard to concentrate on

Wohlfarth's ramblings. Her husband wouldn't be one bit pleased if she went back to work. He'd got used to her being at home all day, making sure there was always a beer in the fridge and that his underpants were nicely folded in his drawer. At the same time, the extra money would come in handy. Three of their beach chairs had been swept out to sea in the last storm. But what use were they anyway when there were no holidaymakers any more? She sighed loudly.

'And what do you think, Frau Paulsen?' asked Wohlfarth, annoyed at this interruption.

'You're quite right,' said Vibke Paulsen, nodding her head vigorously. 'Making children happy is …'

'… the most honourable task that a person can devote themselves to,' Wohlfarth completed the sentence.

Sven-Ole understood only one word of this: task.

'I'd be delighted to have something to do other than carting sheep to the mainland,' he said.

Wohlfarth sat up. 'Right. From now on, you are all working for me again.'

Ramona Bottle cast an irritated look around the room.

'What am I supposed to write your letters with, Herr Wohlfarth?'

The little desk behind which she had sat for many years attending to the business correspondence was bare. No computer, not even a typewriter on it.

'I didn't see any trucks outside, boss,' said Sven-Ole. 'Just the little pick-up.'

'And will you be employing people to sew?' asked Vibke Paulsen. 'Only my niece has been looking for something for ages –'

Wohlfarth made a dismissive hand gesture. 'No, no, I have obviously not made myself clear. It's not about producing toys. It's something quite different. It's about a mission! *My* mission!'

Chapter 5

'What would you like for mother's day?' asked Bruno at lunch.

There was spinach ravioli with cheese sauce. He took a second helping. Boxers need their carbohydrates – he knew that. Pasta was just the thing.

'Have you not had enough, darling?' asked his mother with a frown.

'No,' said Bruno, stuffing three ravioli into his mouth all at the same time. He knew what was coming.

'You eat far too quickly. You should wait until the feeling of being full has set in –'

'It takes twenty minutes for your stomach to realise it's full,' said Bruno, licking his lips and finishing the sentence. 'But I don't want to wait that long.'

His mother didn't always seem to wait until her stomach informed her that it was full, either. She wasn't exactly slim.

'What about mother's day?' asked Bruno again. 'Dad will probably buy you flowers, but I could bring you breakfast in bed.'

'Oh, please, no! Last time you did that, everything ended up on the duvet cover. The juice stains never did come out.'

His mother bent over. 'I have only one wish, son. Professor

Griebel said that today is the day it will be decided if you can take part in the recital at the conservatory.'

All of a sudden the spinach ravioli tasted of cardboard.

'Promise me you'll do your best?'

Bruno's stomach rumbled. It rumbled so hard that Bruno had to run to the loo and throw up.

Later that day, Bruno leafed dutifully through the magazine his mother had brought him, as he lay recovering from his stomach upset. *The Young Virtuoso* contained nothing that was of the remotest interest to him: articles about three-year-olds who could play the Moonlight Sonata perfectly. Exercises for the left hand.

He was just about to slam the magazine shut when something caught his eye. Under an ad for gross piano stools he read: *We're looking for the world's worst mother*.

A website address was given where you could download a questionnaire. First prize: four weeks' holidays on an island, no mothers allowed.

Bruno went into his father's room. He turned on the computer, opened the internet browser and typed in the address: www.worldsworstmothers.eek.

The questionnaire was four pages long. Bruno printed it out and took it into his bedroom. He quickly filled in his name, age and address, and the question *Why do you think your mother is the world's worst mother?* was not difficult to answer.

Because she forces me to play the piano, but I would much rather box, wrote Bruno.

Then it started to get difficult. He had to give all these details about his mother, whether she had relatives and, if so, what they were called, what her likes and dislikes were, how many people were in the household and what kind of pets they had.

When it came to likes, he mentioned her favourite perfume, but for dislikes, he put, *She doesn't like being contradicted.*

My great-aunt Adelheid was first viola, Bruno scribbled under the heading 'Relations'.

He was supposed to send a photo of his mother along with the questionnaire. The only one he could find was taken on his first day at school. She hadn't changed much, apart from getting a bit heavier.

She's a bit fatter than in the picture, wrote Bruno on the back of the photo. Then he folded the questionnaire and put it into an envelope with the photograph. Finally, he wrote the PO box-number address on the outside of the envelope and went and got a stamp.

He didn't really think he'd win first prize. There must be worse mothers than his. But it had done him good to write down what he had to put up with. Now all he had to do was post the letter.

❋

Emily found a note on the kitchen table: *Back later. There are roast potatoes in the fridge. You can have fromage frais with them.*

The potatoes had been there for three days and had got hard around the edges. Emily held the bowl under her nose. It didn't smell good. She got a packet of fromage frais out of the fridge and opened it. There was a furry green film on it. Not surprising, considering that the best-before date had passed in January. Her mother always said you didn't need to pay too much attention to those dates, that most food would keep for much longer. Well, that might be true of things like sugar or tinned tomatoes, but obviously not of dairy products.

Emily opened the larder. It was full of bottles and jars with hot sauces and pastes. Her mother spread stuff like this on her bread for breakfast, even. Emily didn't like spicy foods. She took out a packet of cornflakes, shook the cereal into a bowl and then went into the bathroom to wash her hands.

A red light on the washing machine showed that the wash cycle had finished. Emily's mother had done a wash the previous evening, including Emily's new blouse with the ruffles. Had she not hung the things up yet?

Emily opened the drum. Of course, her mother had, as usual, stuffed far too many things in. Emily pulled a crumpled piece of flowered material out of a tangle of towels, knickers and socks. She tried in vain to smooth it out. The blouse had shrunk by at least two sizes, and the soft and flimsy material had gone hard and stiff. Emily sat down on the toilet seat, pressed the damp remains to her eyes and sobbed.

Her father had given her the blouse as a present on the last father-daughter day they'd had. It had actually been far too expensive, but so lovely. Her father had thought so too.

'Made in India,' her mother had remarked snidely, looking at the label. 'That'll have to be washed first. It's sure to be full of harmful chemicals.' She was clearly annoyed about the blouse because it was a present from Emily's father. 'So much money for such a little scrap of material. It would have been much more sensible to buy you a new pair of runners.'

But Emily didn't want something sensible. The blouse had been lovely, and now there was nothing for it but to throw it out.

She blew her nose on a piece of toilet paper and hauled the rest of the washing out of the machine to hang it up in the kitchen.

Her mother was always forgetting to take the washing out of the machine, just as she had forgotten to take the fromage frais out of the fridge. Emily loved her mother, but it was exhausting to live with her.

When she had hung up the washing, Emily sat at the table to eat her cornflakes. That was when she noticed what it said on the back of the packet: *Fun and games on the beach.* There were pictures of children making sandcastles and young people playing volleyball. Emily would have loved to go to the sea. But this year she was going to have to stay at home again because there was no money for a holiday.

Emily sighed. If only her mother hadn't been so terrible, her father would never have fallen in love with this other woman and they'd all be still together. *And I wouldn't have to eat dusty old cornflakes for lunch*, thought Emily, just as her eyes fell on this sentence: *Wanted: The world's worst mother.*

Well, if that wasn't just the thing!

❁

Sophie was standing in the kitchen stirring a cake mixture. Tomorrow was mother's day, and she wanted to surprise her mother with a home-made Swiss roll. Her mother was quite a good baker but she'd never had the nerve to try Swiss roll. Sophie thought it wasn't really all that difficult. You just had to separate the eggs and beat the whites until they were good and stiff and then mix them carefully into the mixture. It looked wonderful, very light and pale yellow. Suddenly a hand appeared and, quick as lightning, a mucky finger was dabbling in the mixture.

'Nicholas!' yelled Sophie. 'Take your finger out!'

'What's it going to be?' asked Nicholas, licking his finger. 'Pudding?'

'No, it's going to be a mother's day cake,' said Sophie, raising the bowl up over her head. 'Now get lost.'

'But I want to bake a cake too,' said Nicholas.

'Why don't you paint a pretty picture for Mum?' suggested Sophie, taking the bowl to the counter. 'Pass me the sugar. It's there on the table.'

Nicholas gave her a container.

'Not the salt, you twit! Just think, if I'd poured that in!'

'Then there'd be trouble!' Nicholas giggled and ran out of the kitchen.

He'd done it on purpose! But Sophie decided not to make a fuss, not after the row there'd been yesterday. Sophie had come home from school and immediately she'd noticed that her bedroom door was open. There was a big notice on the door since the near catastrophe with the sand: *Absolutely no little brothers allowed!* She'd stuck a photo of Nicholas under the notice and crossed it out with a red marker. Her mother had got into a terrible tizzy about it, but George had only laughed and said, since Nicholas couldn't read properly, one had to resort to such measures.

There had been a vase of flowers that Sophie had picked on her bedside table. The vase had been knocked over, water had spilled over Sophie's diary and the flowers lay strewn about the floor.

Naturally she'd immediately suspected Nicholas. She went into his room, full of a cold anger. He was sitting on the floor, zooming toy cars over the carpet. Without saying a word, she pulled him up by the arm and gave him a resounding clip on the ear. Nicholas stared at her, horrified, and for a moment Sophie was sorry.

Then he started to yell. 'Sofa hit me! Sofa hit me!' he shrieked.

Her mother came at a run.

'What's wrong now? Can I not get a second's peace in this house?'

Nicholas didn't have to say a thing. The finger marks on his cheek were a dead giveaway.

'Sophie! How could you?' Her mother looked at her with almost as much horror as Nicholas had.

'He was in my room and he knocked over the vase of flowers and now everything is wet, even my diary.' It all came pouring out of Sophie.

'In the first place, Nicholas was at playschool all morning, and secondly, I told you yesterday not to put the flowers by your bed because you can get a headache from that, and in the third place, Lulu snuck into your room with me when I went in earlier to open your window. It was very stuffy in there.'

Lulu! Of course. The cat was very keen on flowers. She was always sticking her paws into flower vases. Sophie stood there like a muppet. She was just about to say sorry to Nicholas when her mother said, 'No television for you, starting right now!'

'But today it's –'

'I don't care what's on. You smacked your little brother in the face. That really is the end. And by the way, if you don't comb your hair, I'm going to cut it!'

Sophie left the room without a word.

Then, as she was trying to dry her diary with kitchen paper, a flattened moth fell out of it. One of Nicholas's collection of dead animals. So there! But Sophie knew her mother would never believe her. She was still cross with Sophie and only spoke to her when it was absolutely necessary. That was worse than if she'd shouted at her. But if Sophie could make a good job of this Swiss roll and bring it to her mother in bed on Sunday morning, then surely she'd be forgiven. She spread the mixture on the well-oiled baking tin and stuck it in the oven.

Lulu had jumped up onto the counter and was licking the mixing bowl. Sophie got the cream out of the fridge. She had to beat this now with caster sugar and grated lemon peel, and use it to fill the roll. Easy peasy. She hoped she'd get it done before her mother got home. She'd gone shopping with George. George had promised Sophie he'd make the shopping trip last as long as he could.

But just as Sophie was spreading the lemon cream on the sponge, she heard the key in the lock. Her mother came storming into the kitchen and threw her bag angrily onto a chair. Sophie looked enquiringly at George but he was raising his hands apologetically.

'What's that supposed to be?' asked Sophie's mother, pointing at the baking tray.

'Sofa is making a cake,' said Nicholas, trundling into the kitchen. 'Big fat mama cake.'

'So I see,' said their mother in disgust. 'I hope it's not for me.'

'I thought, since tomorrow is mother's day …'

'Forget it! I'm on a diet for the next two weeks!'

'She's been trying on bikinis,' said George, rolling his eyes.

'I don't know what they've done with the sizes,' said Sophie's mother. 'Last year, a 38 fitted me comfortably.'

Sophie looked at her mother. She wished she were half as slim.

'So you don't want any of the lemon Swiss roll?'

'For heaven's sake, after that I'd look like –' She broke off.

'Like me, you were going to say, weren't you?'

Sophie took the baking tray and threw the contents into the bin.

In her room, she turned on her PC and logged in to Allfriends. Dragon Monster had written, *I think this might interest you. Check out www.worldsworstmothers.eek.*

Chapter 6

Kruschke was standing on the pier, waiting for the ferry, which had just appeared on the horizon. The sun was shining and the waves were peaked with white foam. Kruschke was sweating in his thick jacket, but no sooner had he taken it off than the breeze picked up and he had to put it back on.

He'd been stuck for thirty years now on this odious island. And for all these years, he'd been putting his abilities to work in the service of others. He'd been exploited, first by Wohlfarth Senior, then by his son. Neither of them had ever appreciated his worth, but that was going to change very soon.

Kruschke touched his reddened eyelid, which was oozing unpleasantly again. That was the fault of the ceaseless wind. When Wohlfarth's mission had come to an end, and in a way that Wohlfarth couldn't even dream of, then Kruschke would move back to the mainland. But he would not go alone. He smiled at the thought.

The ferry was approaching. It wasn't bringing tourists. Who would want to holiday on this boring island? The Dune View guesthouse did have two or three guest rooms but, at best, they were occupied now and again by the staff of the ferry when they got stranded on the island because of stormy weather.

When Wohlfarth's factory had been in full swing, there was more activity. Dealers from all over Germany used to come to Nordfall to see Kruschke's creations for themselves. There'd even been a Chinese man among them once, who'd said he wanted to buy woolly dogs for a big store in Peking. Nothing had come of that, and Kruschke was quite sure this person had only come to spy.

The ship's horn tooted loudly, and now Kruschke could see the delivery van that brought the post along with boxes of food. And it was because of the post that he'd come. Normally, the post was delivered to Dune View and was given out by Herr Lührsen, who ran not only the guesthouse but also the island's post office. But Wohlfarth did not want the letters that he was waiting so impatiently for to fall into the wrong hands.

The ferry berthed. The post van was the first off the boat. The postman stopped in front of Kruschke and rolled down his window, saying, 'Mornin'. I have a whole sack of letters for your boss. He didn't advertise for a wife, did he?' He laughed out loud.

'Something like that,' said Kruschke. 'I'm supposed to pick them up. It's urgent.'

The driver got out and hauled a sack out of the back of the van.

Kruschke grabbed it, threw it onto the flatbed of a little pick-up and drove off.

'That fellow gets weirder and weirder,' murmured the postman and drove the few yards to Dune View, where a nice portion of pickled herring with black bread was waiting for him.

※

'Here you go, boss,' said Kruschke, shaking the contents of the postbag onto Wohlfarth's desk.

'Is that all?' asked Wohlfarth, disappointed.

'There are at least a hundred letters there,' said Kruschke. 'We can't accommodate that many here.'

'Of course not, you dunderhead,' said Wohlfarth, tearing open a letter. 'But I'm only counting on a fifty per cent success rate. Here! Here's one now!' He was unfolding a sheet. '"My mother is the worst of all because she didn't give me a horse for my birthday,"' he read out. 'This is what one Annalena from Buxtehude writes. This mother is not dreadful. She's just sensible. This is no good to us.' Wohlfarth fingered an ink-blotched page. 'This is a Kevin from Potsdam, whose mother is supposed to be the worst because she took his Playstation away. Judging by this fellow's spelling, that was the right thing to do.'

Wohlfarth kept tearing open letters. 'Some of them don't even give a return address,' he ranted. 'And Munich is no good anyway, far too far away. Same with Frankfurt.' He threw two letters unread into the waste-paper basket and slit the next one open.

'What on earth are we supposed to do with a photo like that?' Angrily, he tore up a photograph that showed a woman holding her arm defensively up to her face.

Kruschke said nothing, just stood in front of Wohlfarth's desk till his boss had calmed down.

At last, Wohlfarth sorted the letters into three piles and said, 'I'll make a selection later. Tell the others that I want to see them here at seven sharp.'

'Yessir!'

Kruschke walked across the factory floor, opened an iron door and went down a long passageway to the so-called north wing. The materials store and the washrooms for the workers used to be here. Now half a dozen rooms were empty. Sven-Ole was just dipping a paint roller into a bucket.

'How far have you got?' asked Kruschke.

'I still have to do this room and the two behind,' said Sven-Ole, rolling white paint over the wall. 'Could we not go for something a bit more colourful? It all looks so cold.'

'It's not supposed to be a rest home,' said Kruschke shortly.

'I know, I know,' said Sven-Ole. 'Thinking about colours, I have a good joke. If you strangle a smurf, what colour does he go?'

Kruschke snorted contemptuously. 'Seven sharp in the boss's office, and that's no joke,' he said, leaving the room.

In one of the rooms that had already been painted, Vibke Paulsen was just putting sheets on the beds.

Ramona Bottle was standing beside her, reading out of a book: 'When you are speaking to your child, hunker down to him and look him in the eye.' She knelt down. Then she looked at the book again. 'You should always be on the same level as your child.'

Ramona closed the book and took another from the big pile that she'd stacked up beside her.

'Here it says exactly the opposite. It says you should never be on the same level as your child.' She stood up, her bones creaking. 'I can't make head nor tail of it.'

Vibke Paulsen tapped her forehead knowingly. 'I brought up five children. Common sense is better than any book, no matter how clever it is. That's my opinion.'

ld teach cooking and sewing,' said Ramona Bottle. ' you wouldn't have to bother with any of this stupid theory.'

'How far have you got?' asked Kruschke.

Ramona pointed to the heap of books on child-rearing. On one book, a toothless baby grinned; on another, there was a teenager with braces on their teeth.

'I don't know if I can remember all this stuff. I'm a secretary, not a teacher.'

'I think six beds to a room is too much too ask,' said Vibke Paulsen. 'It looks like a youth hostel in here.'

'It'll be fine,' said Kruschke, moving on.

He wasn't at all sure how fine it was going to be. If he was honest, he was a little anxious. If the whole thing took off and it all went differently from the way Wohlfarth imagined it, what then? They'd all end up in jail, that's what. And that couldn't be allowed to happen. Because then Kruschke wouldn't be able to put *his* plan into action.

He gave a bitter laugh. A school for mother improvement! Only Wohlfarth, with his mother fixation, could think up something like that. Mothers were human and humans were flawed creatures, born to die. A discontinued line, so to speak. How different were his creations! They were not only beautiful, but intelligent – two characteristics that were seldom found together in a person made of flesh and blood.

Kruschke went back into the warehouse area and slipped through a semi-transparent plastic sheet that curtained off a section of the warehouse. There they were – his Annas! Whenever he was troubled by doubts, he went and took a look at them. Each one. From Anna 01 to Anna 25. To an outsider, they all looked exactly the same. But he could tell them apart. Anna 12 had a little dimple in her chin. Anna 07 a tiny mole under her left eye. Anna 25's ears stuck out a little. But they were all very beautiful, with their smooth faces, long blonde hair and slim figures. Each one was wearing a flowery skirt, a white blouse and a light blue cardigan. Ramona Bottle had chosen the clothes, and Kruschke thought they were absolutely spot on: not too old-fashioned and not too modern.

Kruschke patted one of them on the arm, stroked the hair of another. He pulled a seam straight here, buttoned up a cardigan there. He could hardly wait to bring them to life, to give them speech and movement.

None of them could hold a candle to Sarah, of course. His Sarah. Kruschke sighed.

At seven o'clock, the workers gathered in Wohlfarth's office. Sven-Ole was still wearing his paint-spattered overalls and seemed to be the only one who was in good form. Any work was better than transporting bleating sheep to the slaughter.

Wohlfarth drummed his fingers on his desk. 'Has anyone seen Kruschke?'

'He has to fix something,' said Vibke Paulsen.

'I've just thought of a great joke, boss. Kruschke puts me in mind of it,' said Sven-Ole. 'A blonde says to her admirer, "How come you're looking at me so strangely?" The admirer says, "I have an artificial eye." The blonde says, "What's it made of?" "Glass," says the admirer, and the blonde nods. "Oh, yes, of course. After all, you have to be able to see through it."' Sven-Ole slapped himself on the thigh with laughter. 'Isn't that a good one?'

When he saw Kruschke, who had just come in, he said quickly, 'I didn't mean to be offensive.'

'I don't know why blondes are supposed to be so funny,' said Ramona Bottle, twirling a lock of hair.

Wohlfarth didn't seem to have been listening. 'Everything under control, Kruschke?'

'Of course, boss,' said Kruschke, sitting on a little chair and giving Sven-Ole a look that would have killed anyone else.

Wohlfarth's waste-paper basket was overflowing, and on his desk was a pretty small pile of questionnaires.

'OK, well, I've checked them all and there are just seventeen that are at all suitable.'

'That's terrific, boss,' said Sven-Ole.

Ramona Bottle said, 'It's definitely better to start small, don't you think?'

Wohlfarth turned to Kruschke. 'How many Annas have we got?'

'If we include Prototype 3131 –'

'Which is probably lying on some sandbank, frightening the seals,' Wohlfarth interrupted.

'Well, then, it's twenty-five,' said Kruschke as calmly as possible. Only his red face betrayed that he was anything but calm.

'That's good. That means we have a reliable reserve of eight. You never know what might go wrong.'

Wohlfarth pressed the questionnaires into Kruschke's hand. 'You have exactly a week to prepare.'

'A week!' cried Kruschke, horrified. 'It takes at least two days to program each one.'

'One week and not a day longer,' said Wohlfarth. 'If we take any more time, we run the risk that the information in the questionnaires is no longer valid. I want the Annas to be ready for work within ten days at the latest.'

'But … will everyone not notice that these … eh … Annas … are dolls?' asked Vibke Paulsen.

'No way!' Kruschke contradicted her. 'They can do everything that a mother can, only better: cleaning, putting the washing machine on, sticking a ready meal in the microwave …'

'They can't cook?'

'They can boil water, but a proper meal that must be carefully prepared and tasted – well, I'm still working on those sensors. In future, every Anna will be programmed so that they can cook everything from good plain food to five-star cuisine.'

'Cooking is not important,' Wohlfarth interrupted. 'It's enough if the children get their favourite food served up to them, and in most cases that's just pizza or chips. What's much more important is whether your Annas can help the children with their homework.'

'Certainly,' said Kruschke, slightly irritated. 'They know the whole curriculum from first to tenth class. They can even make Christmas decorations and crochet pot holders.'

'And can they read aloud?' asked Vibke Paulsen.

'All my Annas have a built-in character-recognition program. A speech module processes everything and the Annas read in a pleasant voice.'

'Aha,' said Ramona Bottle, though she hadn't understood a word of what he'd said.

'And how do we get these wonderful creatures off the island?' asked Sven-Ole.

'On the *Margarethe,* of course,' said Wohlfarth.

'But then everyone will see!' said Vibke Paulsen. 'What can we tell people?'

'What will people think if they see so many blondes all at

once?' asked Wohlfarth. 'They will think they are models. You should just tell everyone that I've set up a school for models. These ladies are the first ones, leaving us after successful training.'

He turned to Ramona Bottle. 'Is the company sign I ordered ready?'

'It should be here by tomorrow at the latest,' replied Ramona eagerly. 'The letters WIMI in green neon, as requested.'

'What's that supposed to mean?' asked Sven-Ole, slow on the uptake.

'Wohlfarth's Institute for Mother Improvement,' replied Wohlfarth shortly. 'But officially the letters stand for Wohlfart's Institute for Model Instruction.'

'Nobody could ever work out what it *really* means,' said Sven-Ole.

'That's the point,' said Wohlfarth.

'But don't you think there'll be talk when all these women that nobody has ever seen on the island start leaving the factory?' asked Vibke Paulsen.

'We'll just say they wanted to remain anonymous, and anyway, there is nothing less suspicious than attractive blondes.' Wohlfarth laughed.

This rare laugh gave Ramona Bottle the courage to ask the question that nobody had so far asked. 'And what about the other way around? I mean, how are the mothers going to get here?'

'Students, please,' said Wohlfarth. 'Mothers – *proper* mothers, deserving of the title …' He pointed again at the portrait of his mother on the wall. 'They won't be *mothers* until they leave us.'

Looking at the three enquiring faces, it occurred to Wohlfarth that he still hadn't answered their question.

'There is certainly a small logistical problem. We only have one window of six hours while the unfortunate children are at school. In this time frame, the swap must take place.'

'You're not thinking of …' Vibke Paulsen swallowed, 'using force?'

Wohlfarth smiled maliciously and patted the pile of papers. 'Fortunately, that won't be necessary. Every one of them will come here of her own free will. I can assure you of that.'

❈

Kruschke had been working round the clock for the last few days. The programming had proved very difficult. Mechanical functions, such as vacuuming, ironing and making beds, were easy to program: they were the same for all the Annas. What had taken up most of his time had been language. Hopefully he'd overlooked nothing. Kruschke shook his head. No, no. He hadn't made any mistakes. His Annas were absolutely perfect. So perfect that no one would realise what they really were.

And they had survived the first test. Kruschke accompanied them himself to the ferry port. They marched out of Wohlfarth's factory through the gate that had been flung wide and on down the street to the harbour where Wohlfarth's dazzling white motor yacht *Margarethe* was anchored. They took their seats on deck, throwing bright scarves over their heads and putting on their sunglasses.

Bursting with pride, Sven-Ole took up the helm, imagining himself as some big oil magnate or rock star who was speeding off over the Mediterranean to Capri with his playmates. Only the North Sea wasn't the Mediterranean, and Nordfall wasn't Capri.

Even on an island full of beautiful people, the departure of seventeen blondes would have caused something of a stir. All the more so on Nordfall.

Swantje, who did a bit of casual work at Dune View, tore off her apron and exclaimed, 'I want to go to this model school too, if that's what you look like at the end of it!'

And Hinnerk, the last fisherman on the island, who was just unloading his catch at the harbour, couldn't keep his mouth closed, so amazed was he to see seventeen attractive young women going by. He let a whole box of flounder fall back into the sea from sheer astonishment.

The only strange thing was that the young women didn't say a word to each other. They had come silently along the gangway, and silently they sat in the yacht.

'That's what models are like,' declared Swantje. 'They don't talk to each other because they all distrust each other.'

'I couldn't say which one I liked best,' said Hinnerk. 'They were all equally pretty.'

'Well, you can forget it. You'll never get one like that. As long as you stink of fish,' said Swantje, poking Hinnerk in the ribs.

'You smell of cooking fat,' Hinnerk replied, but his grin made it plain that that didn't bother him.

Chapter 7

Bruno was in no hurry to get home on this fine June day. It was Thursday, and the thought of the looming piano lesson with Professor Griebel made him queasy. Of course he hadn't been allowed to take part in the recital. 'The fluency in his left hand leaves much to be desired,' Professor Griebel had explained to his mother. 'He really needs to practise more and to take more lessons. That would give him some chance of making an appearance at our big summer concert.'

As soon as she heard the word 'concert' Bruno's mother's eyes lit up. Since then, Bruno had had to practise every day, whether he wanted to or not. Only when his father came home in the evening and made pained faces, saying, 'I've got a headache,' was Bruno allowed to close the lid of the piano.

There was no point. Even if he played for ten hours a day, he would never amount to anything. Professor Griebel knew this perfectly well. And Bruno was sure of it too. He suspected the professor of deliberately giving his mother to understand that her son could one day be an important pianist. The money he made from Bruno he surely spent on taking that red-haired girl student out to dinner.

Bruno kicked a tin can angrily against a lamp post. Suppose

he was injured? Maybe he could catch his hand in the door. His friend Jim had done that – not on purpose, of course. And now his right hand was all bandaged up.

'You can have my punchbag, if you like,' Jim had said. 'I can't train for the next four weeks.'

That was a very tempting offer. But the punchbag was far too big for Bruno to be able to sneak it into the house. The only way was for Bruno to go around to Jim's place and use the punchbag there. As far as his parents were concerned, he was going to his friend's house to help him with his maths.

Bruno opened the gate and was slouching up the neatly weeded path when he heard a voice trilling, 'Ah, here comes dear Bruno!'

Bruno looked up in amazement. A strange woman was standing in the open doorway, wearing a silly apron and beaming at him.

'What ... what are you ... doing here?' stuttered Bruno.

The woman came towards him and before Bruno knew what was happening she'd taken his schoolbag from him. 'It's terribly heavy. Come in, my dear. I've made your favourite food. You do like oven-fresh chips with ketchup and mayonnaise, don't you?'

Prattling away, the woman went ahead of Bruno into the house. Puzzled, he followed her.

There was a wonderful smell of oven chips in the kitchen. Bruno's mouth watered. Was it all a dream?

'Who are you?' he asked.

The woman, who was just opening the oven door, turned to him. 'I'm your Aunt Anna, of course! Don't you recognise me?'

Bruno frowned. He didn't know any Aunt Anna.

'I'm a second cousin of Great-aunt Adelheid.'

Bruno did know Great-aunt Adelheid. The one with the viola.

'I've met her,' he said. 'At my grandmother's birthday. There were these totally delicious cheesecakes. Great-aunt Adelheid played something for us and we weren't allowed to eat until she'd finished.'

'Every birthday was like that,' the young woman cried. 'She sawed away for ever and it was dire, right?' She smiled conspiratorially at Bruno.

Bruno smiled back. She wasn't half bad, this aunt. 'But I don't remember you,' he said.

Aunt Anna piled crispy chips onto a plate. 'How would you? The last time I saw you, you were only a baby. But I thought maybe your mum had shown you photos.'

The only photos that Bruno's mother ever showed him were ones of him sitting at the piano. He sighed.

Aunt Anna squeezed ketchup out of a bottle onto his chips and pushed the plate towards him. 'Enjoy your food, my dear.'

Bruno was just about to stick a forkful of food in his mouth when he suddenly lowered the fork and asked, 'And where's Mum?'

Aunt Anna sat down beside him at the table.

'She's gone to the North Sea, for her health.'

'She never mentioned it to me,' said Bruno.

'Oh, you know, she's been meaning to go to this spa for ages. And then a place suddenly became available. She had to decide immediately. So she called me and asked if I could look after you for a while.'

Bruno chewed thoughtfully. It was true that his mother had been saying for ages that she needed to go to a health farm. That was something his parents were always arguing about, because his father said she needed no such thing, that, after all, she was at home all day and had no stress.

'But the housekeeping, the garden, the ironing – and Bruno. I have all these things to worry about,' she had always replied.

Now she had nothing to worry about.

'And how long will she be away?' asked Bruno, putting one of the crispiest chips into his mouth.

'Four weeks,' said Aunt Anna.

Bruno tried not to look too happy, but he couldn't manage it. He was beaming all over his face.

❀

Sophie wasn't in much of a hurry to get home either. The letter would have come today. The letter from school to say that she was going to have to repeat a year at school. Her mother would definitely have read it by now, and the thought of what she would say made Sophie go weak at the knees.

Opening the street door, she saw that their mail box hadn't been emptied. Odd. As she opened it, an advertising flyer, a mail-order catalogue and several letters fell out. The school used grey, environment-friendly envelopes. And there was one of those. Sophie took it and wondered briefly if she shouldn't just make it disappear. But that wouldn't alter the fact that she had to repeat the year. Better to face the music. She went up to their apartment and opened the door.

'Mum? Mum, I have something to tell you, but please, please, don't be angry …' She broke off. A woman in an awful skirt and an even worse cardigan was standing in the hallway.

'Hello, my dear. How tall you've got! And what lovely hair you have!'

Nobody had ever said that to her before. Sophie's hair was thick and curly and, no matter what she did, she always looked as if something had exploded on her head.

She shook her hair a bit and then said, 'Excuse me, but I don't know who you are.'

'I'm your Aunt Anna. Don't you remember?'

Sophie didn't remember any Aunt Anna, but her skirt didn't seem quite so awful any more.

'I'm a cousin of your father's. Your mother and I used to be great friends, but since the separation –' Aunt Anna broke off and sighed. 'You must know how difficult that all was. But still, when she needed to leave so suddenly, she thought of me. Here, she left you a note.'

Aunt Anna took a piece of paper out of her pocket.

Had to go away, all a bit of a surprise, explain later. Kisses, Mum, read Sophie.

She was relieved. A narrow escape. But for how long? Four weeks? Had Aunt Anna just said something about four weeks?

'It takes four weeks, this treatment.'

'Treatment?' asked Sophie, astonished.

'I don't mean that she's ill. It's just a health farm, you know. You go there to lose weight and relax.'

'She never mentioned anything like that.'

'Maybe not to you,' said Aunt Anna. 'But she'll have discussed it with George, wouldn't you think?'

Sophie nodded. Her mother discussed lots of things with George that Sophie only found out about by chance. For example, that they were planning a cycling trip along the Elbe this summer. Sophie hated cycling.

'What time does Nicholas have to be picked up from his crèche?' asked Aunt Anna.

'Half past three,' said Sophie.

'Wonderful!' crowed Aunt Anna. 'We'll have a bit of calm before the storm, then.'

Really, that ugly blue cardigan wasn't so bad, Sophie thought. It went well with her blonde hair.

Lulu came out of the kitchen and rubbed against Aunt Anna's legs. She didn't react but prattled cheerfully on. 'I do like little children, you know, but they can be terribly irritating. Don't you agree, Sophie?'

'Stop that, Lulu!' cried Sophie, as the cat raised her paws to scratch Aunt Anna's flawless leg.

'What am I supposed to stop?' asked Aunt Anna.

'I didn't mean you, I meant the cat.'

Sophie pointed at Lulu, who was getting up on her hind legs, to get a sniff at Aunt Anna's skirt.

Aunt Anna looked down. She seemed a little dismayed. Maybe she didn't like cats.

'That's Lulu,' said Sophie.

Aunt Anna smiled broadly. 'How lovely. Delighted to make your acquaintance, Lulu!'

❈

Emily opened the door to the flat. It was empty. As expected. In the kitchen, there was a note on the table.

A miracle has happened! Will be in touch soon. Love, Mum.

Emily sat down. If you didn't know her mother, you might think the note had been written in great haste, the way the letters seemed to fly over the paper, slanting severely to the right as if they were trying to take shelter from a fierce downpour. But her mother always wrote like that. Because as she wrote, something else usually occurred to her, something she absolutely must attend to.

The doorbell rang. Emily peered through the spyhole. There was a woman on the other side of the door. She looked quite nice.

Emily opened the door. 'What can I do for you?'

'It's me,' said the woman. 'Aunt Anna.'

Emily frowned. She didn't know any Aunt Anna. But maybe it was a friend of her mother's.

'My mother is not at home,' said Emily.

The woman put a foot in the door.

'Of course not, my dear. I know that. That's why I'm here.'

Chapter 8

Kruschke was back at the ferry port. It was calm today. A few clouds hung listlessly in a blue sky. The sea was dark grey and it was as smooth and motionless as satin.

The Annas had all left early that morning, and now the women who were to become super-slim, super-blonde models were expected.

Nordfall's inhabitants hadn't been all that interested in the transformation of a toy factory into a modelling school. Only Jens Lührsen, the owner of Dune View, had been excited. He would be delivering lunch every day for the models. His wife, Ilse, soon put paid to his good mood, though.

'There won't be much business there,' she remarked. 'You know what those young ladies live on: low-fat yoghurt, celery sticks and mineral water.'

But as they watched the women disembarking, she said, 'It will be some job to turn that lot into anything decent.' And Swantje, who was watching with her, had to agree.

'That fat one in front needs to lose at least thirty kilos. That'll take her a year.'

Quite unlike the silent ladies who had left the island earlier that morning, these ones were chattering so loudly that they drowned out even the screeching of the seagulls. Sentences like 'This is ridiculous!' and 'I want to speak to the organiser immediately!' were to be heard.

'They all seem a bit cross,' whispered Swantje to the manageress of Dune View.

'You're right there. Look at that one with the grown-out perm – she's going to explode with anger.'

A little roundy woman who was pulling a pink trolley behind her came surprisingly quickly down the gangway and called: 'Where is Clang Clang, the world-famous virtuoso?'

Kruschke ran up to her and took her by the arm. 'You are Bruno's mother, aren't you? Please be patient for a moment. It will all become clear.'

'Become clear?' spat the woman, who had got quite red in the face. 'What is there to become clear?' She took a letter out of her bag. 'I have been informed that the world-famous pianist Clang Clang wanted to meet me here to discuss my son's future. He considers him unusually talented.'

The other women had come closer by now and they surrounded Kruschke. They were all waving letters.

'I was invited to an interview for a job as a senior bookkeeper,' cried a woman with wild red hair.

A very fat lady pushed herself forward.

'I was supposed to take part in a trial for a new weight-loss product. Lose twenty kilos in three days or get ten thousand euro compensation. Give me the stuff!'

'No, I was first,' cried another woman.

'You can't want to lose weight, you stick insect,' shouted the fat woman.

'You haven't seen me in a bikini,' replied the thin woman.

Kruschke had his hands full trying to calm the ladies down. At last, he got them to follow him into Wohlfarth's factory.

'Like a flock of gobbling geese,' said Ilse Lührsen and she went back into Dune View, shaking her head. She had a lot to do. Wohlfarth had ordered seventeen portions of fish fillet for that evening. With cucumber salad.

Wohlfarth had written a speech. He was walking up and down the factory floor, memorising it.

'Ladies … No, that's too stiff. And anyway, they are not ladies. Well, then, my dear mothers … Rubbish, that's precisely what they are *not*. Otherwise, they wouldn't be here. What'll I call them?'

At that moment, the gate was flung open and a pack of enraged women came charging into the building. They were all shouting each other down.

'Are you responsible for this circus?' called a long scrawny person in a flowing garment of indeterminate colour.

'If you haven't got a good explanation, I will call the police,' screamed a fat little woman, gesturing threateningly with a mobile phone.

Wohlfarth raised his hands defensively.

'Quiet, ladies, please. Silence, please.' He pointed at a couple of rows of chairs. 'At least sit down and have something to eat.'

As if to order, Ramona Bottle and Vibke Paulsen appeared with coffee pots, cups and plates of goodies.

The long scrawny one shook her head. 'I only drink barley coffee.'

And the short fat one asked, 'Are those low-calorie biscuits?'

'Oh, yes,' said Vibke Paulsen. 'Don't worry. We've thought of everything. There's ordinary coffee and decaffeinated and herbal teas, low-calorie biscuits and soya milk …'

She was dishing out cups and plates and speaking soothingly to everyone, and gradually peace descended.

The seventeen women were now sitting quietly on their chairs, looking expectantly at Wohlfarth.

He cleared his throat a couple of times and then he began. 'You are surely wondering why you are here, and I will tell you all in a moment. But on the voyage over, you may have gathered a few things. You are all mothers, and …' Wohlfarth took a deep breath, 'and you are all dreadful mothers. To be quite clear: not only are you dreadful mothers, you are the world's worst mothers.'

A storm of indignation broke out.

'Are you crazy?' one woman yelled, and another cried, 'This has to be *Candid Camera*. Cooey!' She waved and grinned all around.

'No, no, you've got it all wrong,' said Wohlfarth. 'Let me explain –'

But they wouldn't let him. The short fat one was thumbing her mobile. 'Hello? Hello? Is that the police?'

Then she lowered the mobile. 'Nothing.'

'Unfortunately, we don't get a signal here on Nordfall,' said Vibke Paulsen.

The tumult got louder. 'I'm going. I'm not putting up with this,' cried a lady in an elegant suit with carefully coiffured hair.

'That's right. I must get home, my Timmy will be home from school at any moment,' said the short fat one.

'Please listen for a moment,' said Wohlfarth, unfolding a sheet of paper. 'I would like to read something to you, and I think you will be very happy to stay here after you have heard it.'

He cleared his throat and read. '"My mother is so suspicious. She reads my diary secretly. And the first thing she does when she gets home is to check if the TV is still warm, because I'm not allowed to watch telly. It makes you stupid, she claims. But she watches all sorts of rubbish every night till really late. If I say I'm meeting a friend, she rings up to make sure it's true. She'd love to be able to get me implanted with one of those chips, so she could track my every move."'

Wohlfarth broke off. 'I don't think I need to read any more, do I?'

The woman in the chic suit, whose pointy nose had got very white, took out a handkerchief and snorted noisily into it.

Wohlfarth took a new sheet.

'This will interest one of you for sure: "My mother is the world's worst mother because she forces me to play the piano, though I'd much prefer to box. I can't play at all. And I'm always terrified of my piano lesson, especially since I've been going to Professor Griebel. He's mad expensive, and I wish my mother would save the money, but I just can't talk to her. If I say anything, she immediately bursts into tears and that makes me feel guilty. And all because Great-aunt Adelheid used to play the viola. But that doesn't necessarily make me musical, does it???" There are three question marks here,' said Wohlfarth, lowering the page.

The woman with the grown-out perm leapt up and cried, 'But it's not true. You should hear Bruno! I played Mozart to him in the womb! And in preschool he could play 'Twinkle, Twinkle' on the recorder and –'

'What you have to say does not interest me in the slightest,' said Wohlfarth coldly. 'All I am interested in is what your children have to say. This one, for example: "I'm ten, but my mother treats me like a baby. I'm not even allowed to go to my friend's house by myself, and he only lives around the corner. And even if it's warm outside, I have to wear my scarf and gloves. Everyone laughs at me and calls me a mammy's boy. I'm not allowed to go to the playground with the others either, because I might break something."'

The short fat one gave a loud sob. 'But you should have seen Timmy when he was born. He was so tiny!' She indicated the size of a hamster with her hands.

Wohlfarth would not be distracted. He read on and on. At the end, seventeen women sat and stared at the ground. None of them dared to look at her neighbour, so unpleasant was all that they'd heard.

'But why are we here now?' asked a woman who had so far kept quiet. She was tanned and muscular. When she opened her mouth, you could see that she had a piercing in her tongue.

'Have you seen those letters on the building?' asked Wohlfarth. 'WIMI. Can you think what that might mean?'

Most of them shook their heads.

'It means Wohlfarth's Institute for Mother Improvement. Wohlfarth is me, and the mothers – that's you.'

Chapter 9

Bruno gave a punch. Whammm! And again. Wham! Wham! The punchbag swung to and fro. Bruno had to duck to avoid getting it in the face. Then he jumped up, danced around the punchbag and gave another punch. He felt strong. He felt alive. And most of all, he felt happy.

He had hung Jim's punchbag on the thickest branch of the oak tree. Now he boxed the punchbag with a series of faster, lighter punches.

'Bruno!' called a voice. 'Bruno, there was a phone call for you.'

Aunt Anna came along the garden path towards him. She was carrying a tray with a glass of strawberry-flavoured milk on it.

'You need something to keep your strength up,' she said, smiling at Bruno.

She was always smiling. At first, Bruno had found it a bit irritating. But he'd got used to it.

'Who phoned?' he asked 'Mum?'

'No. Your piano teacher.'

Bruno went ice-cold. Today was Thursday, and he had genuinely forgotten that he should have been at his piano lesson. He hadn't played the piano for a week. Actually, since Aunt Anna had been in the house. She had closed the lid of the piano, locked it and thrown the key down the toilet. Bruno had stood helplessly by. How could she do a thing like that?

'Now you don't need to feel guilty for not playing,' she'd said.

Bruno's father didn't know a thing about all this. He had been pretty surprised when he came home that first evening to find, not his wife, but a complete stranger. He'd tried to phone Bruno's mother on her mobile.

'Of course, all I'm getting is the voicemail,' he'd cried. 'Isn't that just typical!' But his anger soon dissolved when he saw what Aunt Anna served up for supper. Steak that was still bloody, with potato wedges dripping with fat. Bruno's mother never cooked anything like that. Aunt Anna hadn't prepared the meal herself. She'd got it from a nearby steakhouse

'I can't cook a thing,' she'd confided to Bruno. 'But don't give me away.'

Bruno never let on. Nor had he told his father that Aunt Anna never ate with him. She was probably on a diet. His mother was always doing that, and then in between meals she stuffed herself with chocolates and cake. Women were just weird.

With Aunt Anna's arrival, a whole new life had begun. After she'd thrown the key of the piano down the loo, she'd said, 'I've heard that you are a very good boxer. Do you want to show me?'

Bruno had borrowed Jim's punchbag, and since then he'd been training every day. And every day he was getting better and better.

On the third day, a postcard had come from his mother, with a picture of a seagull on the front.

My dears,
Don't worry, I'm very well. I'm enjoying the sea air and
I'm looking forward to seeing you in four weeks' time.

Bruno wasn't in the least bit worried about his mother, but about something else entirely.

'What did Professor Griebel say?' he asked anxiously now.

'He asked if you would be coming today.'

'And what did you tell him?'

'I said that you wouldn't be coming today, or tomorrow, or ever again.'

Bruno didn't know whether to laugh or cry.

'Mum will explode when she finds out,' he said.

Aunt Anna's smile got wider.

'Don't fret, my dear. You won't know your mother when she comes home.'

Bruno often thought back to these words later.

❋

'Would you like something to drink or maybe a few biscuits?'

Aunt Anna was standing in the door of Sophie's room, passing her in a tray.

'Super! Thank you,' said Sophie and bit into a cookie.

'Enjoy!' said Aunt Anna and disappeared again.

No 'When are you going to tidy your room?' or 'Have you done your homework?' No complaints that she had forgotten, yet again, to empty the dishwasher or to put the clean clothes in the wardrobe. No orders to comb her hair or not to chew her nails. Since Aunt Anna had been in the house, Sophie had all the time in the world.

She licked the biscuit crumbs from her fingers and logged in to Allfriends.

Dragon Monster had written to her: *Hey, how are things? Everything OK with you?*

Sophie answered: *Better than OK. My mum is gone to a health farm, and our auntie is looking after us. My stepfather wasn't too pleased at first, because Mum had said nothing to him, but I think he likes Aunt Anna too. My mum's probably gone to one of those wellness thingies where you can lose weight too. And do you know the best thing? Aunt Anna is the first one that Nicholas hasn't been able to wind around his little finger. He can cry buckets, as much as he likes. She just looks kindly at him and says nothing. Then he totally explodes. She's super nice to me. Never nags if my room is not tidy, lets me listen to as much music as I like and to spend as long as I like online.*

Dragon Monster wrote back: *Hey, send that auntie over to me, sounds really cool.*

The door burst open and Nicholas came in. 'When's Mummy coming home?' he asked for about the hundredth time.

'I told you. She's gone to a health farm and she'll be back in three weeks.'

'What's a health farm?' Nicholas wanted to know.

'It's like going on your holidays,' said Sophie.

'Will you read it to me again?' Nicholas pressed a thoroughly crumpled postcard into Sophie's hand.

'You must know it off by heart by now,' said Sophie. 'Oh, well. "Dear George, dear Nicholas, dear Sophie."' It always irked her that she came last in the list. '"It's lovely here and I'm relaxing hugely. Lots of love from Mum/Marie."'

She'd scribbled in the margin: *Give Nicholas a kiss from me.*

So far, Sophie had left that bit out when she read the card to Nicholas, but he looked so miserable now that she said, 'Oh look, here's another bit that I never saw before. It says: Give Nicholas a kiss from me.'

Nicholas turned a tear-stained and dirt-smeared cheek towards her. Sophie hesitated for a moment, and then she bent down and gave him a quick kiss.

'You have to kiss me properly,' said Nicholas. 'It has to smack, like this.' Nicholas made a loud smacking sound with his tongue.

'Wash your face first, and then we'll see,' said Sophie.

'You're so mean!' Nicholas stomped out of the room.

Sophie was about to write to Dragon Monster to tell him what songs she'd just bought, which ones she wanted to buy and which ones she was not sure if she should buy or not, when Nicholas reappeared. With a clean face this time.

'Will you kiss me now?' he asked.

At that moment, Aunt Anna came into the room. 'You shouldn't be disturbing your sister. Out you go!'

'But Sofa is supposed to give me a kiss. Mama said so, look!' He reached the card with the seagull out to Aunt Anna.

'Your mum's gone to a health farm and she's very well,' said Aunt Anna. 'Come on, now.'

She took Nicholas and dragged him, screaming, out of the room.

Sophie almost had a guilty conscience. But after all, it was only fair that for once things were not going Nicholas's way.

The next day, Aunt Anna went a bit too far.

Nicholas usually got a sticky, sweet cereal with milk for breakfast.

'It doesn't taste nice,' he said, pushing the bowl away.

George, who was in an awful hurry, knocked over a cup of coffee as he stood up, looking at the clock.

'What doesn't taste nice?'

'Those aren't Honey-Bunnies. It tastes terrible.'

Sophie looked into Nicholas's bowl and nearly burst out laughing.

'It's Lulu's cat crunchies. Aunt Anna, what have you done?'

Aunt Anna, who, as usual, was not sitting with them at the table, but was bustling around the kitchen in an apron, armed with a dishcloth, pulled a packet off cat food off the shelf and said, 'Nicholas always has this, and Sophie and George have that.' She pointed at a packet of sliced bread.

'I have to go,' said George. 'Will you please explain to Anna the difference between cat food and child food.'

Aunt Anna was still standing smiling with the packet of cat food in her hand. Sophie stood up and took it out of her hand.

'This is for Lulu, and this,' she pointed at the Honey-Bunnies, '*this* is for Nicholas.'

She spoke as if she were talking to an illiterate person. Which Aunt Anna was not – she could read. On the first evening, she'd read aloud to Nicholas. Even if it was in an extraordinary monotone. Nicholas didn't want to be read to by her after that. He found her voice 'creepy'.

When George had no time – and he often had no time – Sophie had to read to Nicholas. And it wasn't nearly as bad as she thought it would be. When you read to him, Nicholas was very quiet. He didn't fidget, he didn't whine, he snuggled into Sophie, he sucked his security blanket and just listened.

Now he was sitting at the kitchen table with his arms pressed close to him, staring darkly into his bowl. Sophie took it away and put it down for Lulu, who went at it with a lot of slurping.

'When you were very small, you used to swipe the crunchies out of Lulu's bowl. You used to like them,' said Sophie.

'But I'm not small now,' said Nicholas crossly.

'You are a little boy and you must be good and do what your big sister says,' warbled Aunt Anna.

Even Sophie thought that was a bit much.

'Come on, Nicholas,' she said. 'I don't have to be in school until the second lesson. I can take you to school first.'

She stood up from the table.

'Could you make a sandwich for Nicholas's break, Aunt Anna?'

George usually made a sandwich for Nicholas to take to preschool, but today he'd forgotten.

'Of course. What would you like? Salami, cheese, jam, butter?' Aunt Anna took two slices of bread out of the packet.

'One with cheese and one with salami, as always,' said Sophie. 'And with butter, of course.'

Sophie put her plate into the dishwasher and looked out of the corner of her eye as Aunt Anna put a slice of cheese on the bread, smeared the butter over the cheese, and then put a second slice of bread on top. Usually, people do it the other way around, thought Sophie. Oh, well, what did it matter, it came to the same thing.

But one thing was clear. Aunt Anna was definitely not a good housekeeper.

❀

Emily was lying on the sofa on her tummy watching television. There was a report on the North Frisian Islands. She saw the islands of Pellworm, Amrum, Föhr and Sylt. Which of these islands was her mother on right now? Aunt Anna had just said that she was on an island in the North Sea for her health. On the coffee table was the postcard that Emily had got from her mother. There was a seagull on it, but she hadn't put her address. Hardly surprising, considering how scatterbrained she was.

The postmark gave nothing away. Emily turned the card this way and that. There was something funny about it. The words?

Dear Emmykins,

I'm sure you were surprised that I left so suddenly, but I'm fine and I'm making progress.

Mum.

Progress? In what? In relaxation? Hopefully. Maybe everything would be easier if her mother had four weeks with nothing to think about. No interviews, no car threatening to fall to pieces at any moment, no daughter.

Emily turned up the television.

Aunt Anna went on hoovering. That was her favourite thing. She was eternally going over the flat with the vacuum cleaner. She even hoovered the tables and shelves. Yesterday Emily had only just rescued a piece of paper out of the machine. Her mother had written important addresses on it – the doctor, the mechanic and so on. Emily had put the paper carefully into her pocket so that it couldn't disappear into the belly of the vacuum cleaner. She pulled it out now and smoothed it with her hand. And suddenly it came to her what was wrong with the postcard. The handwriting.

Emily laid the piece of paper with the addresses and the postcard side by side. In the addresses, her mother had made mistakes. She'd scratched things out, scribbled things in between the lines, underlined some things. The handwriting on the postcard was her handwriting, yes. Emily recognised the little circles that her mother made instead of dots over the letter i. But she never wrote as neatly as this. Was that a sign of relaxation? Emily wanted to hear it from the woman herself.

'Anna!' she called over the noise of the vacuum cleaner. 'Aunt Anna!'

Aunt Anna did not react. Emily stood up from the sofa and went out into the hallway. She pulled out the plug.

'The hoover is broken,' said Aunt Anna, looking down the tube.

'I pulled out the plug,' Emily explained. 'Could you please give me Mum's telephone number? I'd like to phone her.'

Aunt Anna smiled. 'She has no signal.'

'Of course not,' said Emily. 'She hasn't even got her mobile with her.'

When Emily had phoned her mother's number, it had rung in the cutlery drawer.

'She has no signal,' repeated Aunt Anna.

'But there must be a landline where she is.'

'She can't be disturbed. Under no circumstances may she be disturbed. She's very well,' said Aunt Anna. 'She's very, very well.'

Chapter 10

Kruschke rubbed his eyes. He'd spent half the night looking at the screens in the cellar, checking the pictures that his Annas sent to him. He had fitted cameras in their beautiful blue eyes, cameras that allowed him to monitor everything that went on around them. Except at night. Of course, the dolls did not sleep, but they lay down and closed their eyes.

So far, everything had gone without a hitch. Nobody had any suspicions. The only false note had been struck by Anna 13. She had stupidly given that horrid little boy cat food. But Sophie had ticked 'none' in the 'pets' field on the questionnaire. Otherwise he'd have programmed the doll accordingly. So of course Anna 13 didn't have a clue about how to deal with the cat. But if that was the worst thing that happened, he would be quite happy.

Now he just needed to get the mothers a few pretty pictures of their children so they wouldn't be worried. Here was a good one. There was a girl – was she called Emily? Kruschke looked at a sheet of paper. Quite right. So, here was Emily on the sofa watching television and Anna 01 was hoovering away around her.

Anna 05 wasn't doing too badly either. Kruschke chose a scene that showed a boy called Dennis sitting at a table doing his homework. A hand was ruffling his hair, and Dennis raised his head gratefully and looked straight into the camera. Dennis's mother had never had time for that kind of thing. If she wasn't in the gym or out jogging, she was sunbathing. Well, that would soon change.

Oh, no! He quickly pressed the delete key. Nobody must ever see that. Anna 13 was making a sandwich, only she put the butter on the cheese instead of on the bread.

Kruschke looked at his watch. Half past one. High time he was in bed. Tomorrow would be another hard day. None of them had ever imagined how demanding seventeen mothers could be. It was like minding mice at crossroads.

It had started as soon as the rooms were allocated. There were complaints after the first night. Nobody wanted to share a room with Susie, Emily's mother, because she talked in her sleep. Jacqueline, Dennis's mother, got stick for hogging the bathroom for hours in the evening. And everyone fell over her dumb-bells. Katherine, Bruno's mother, complained that she was allergic to goose down. If Vibke Paulsen wasn't so good at smoothing ruffled feathers, the whole thing would have got completely out of hand.

Since classes had started, things had been going better. They began at eight in the morning. At half past twelve they had an hour for lunch. Then class started again, and in the afternoons there were workshops. After dinner in the evening the mothers were allowed to watch television for precisely ninety minutes. There was always a row about what programme to watch.

Kruschke sighed. He was very happy that he only had to deal with the mothers during class time. He taught the correct way to use a motor track and how to build model aeroplanes. Mothers who only had daughters could opt out of these lessons and instead go to Vibke Paulsen to learn how to knit dolly clothes, make soft toys and sew the scariest costumes for Hallowe'en. She also gave lessons in 'how to bake biscuits in such a way that there is as much mixture left over as possible' and 'how to comfort girls going through puberty', and she was in charge of the reading-aloud workshop.

Ramona Bottle, on the other hand, had the thankless task of instructing the mothers in practical theory. In her class they dealt with things like 'raising children in changing times' and 'how do I recognise my child's true self?' Hardly any of them were interested in this, and accordingly it was nothing but bad grades. Only Sophie's mother managed to do well in the subject.

Sven-Ole's classes were everyone's favourite. Not only because he was a relatively young man, but also because he set hardly any homework. He taught the mothers the right way to play badminton and hide and seek, how to draw hopscotch boxes and how to do French skipping. Of course, not an hour went by without him coming up with some silly joke.

Kruschke turned the monitors off and left the room. He was dead tired, but he couldn't go to bed yet. First, he had to pay someone a visit.

✻

Emily's mother, Susie, was standing at her bedroom window, looking out. She saw Kruschke crossing the yard and setting off in the direction of the dunes. What was he going to the sea for in the middle of the night?

Kruschke didn't give the impression of having a special love of nature. But as for her, she loved the sea. No matter what the season – whether it was blue-grey and choppy or turquoise blue and smooth as silk. She'd wanted to go to the seaside with Emily this summer, but as long as she had no job that would just be a pipe dream. And now here she was on this island, missing her daughter dreadfully.

She wondered if Emily missed her too. Probably not, because she was so awful, as Emily had said on the questionnaire. She was probably getting along much better without her.

Wohlfarth had told the mothers that trained carers were looking after their children while they were in the school for mothers. After four weeks, they would get a certificate and then they could go home.

Four whole weeks. Four weeks without Emily's sleepy grumbling when Susie woke her up in the mornings, her chuckles when she was watching cartoons on the television. Of course that was all wrong. Children shouldn't laugh only at the television. Their mothers should make them laugh too. This much Susie had learnt by now. But how? She'd never been able to make Emily laugh. She made her cry, more likely. *I want to improve*, thought Susie. *I really want to be a better mother to Emily.*

If only she wasn't so homesick! She could feel a sob coming, and she put her hand in front of her mouth. But someone was hissing from the bed next to hers, 'Can you please be quiet! I want to sleep.'

Susie tiptoed back to bed as quietly as possible. She pulled Porky out from under her pillow. Porky was the lucky piggy that Emily had made her. 'You must carry it with you always, then it will bring you luck, Mum,' Emily had said. And Porky was the only thing that Susie never lost or mislaid or left behind her some place. But it hadn't exactly brought her loads of luck. She pulled the duvet over her head and let the tears come.

❄

A siren shrieked at seven in the morning. The mothers got up, yawning and stretching. Only one of them had got up before the siren. She'd leapt out of bed and raced into the bathroom so that she could be first in the shower. Two other mothers, in the same white nightshirts with the squiggly letters 'WIMI' on the breast pocket, ran after her.

'Today, I'm going to be first,' cried one of them.

'No, me. I haven't washed my hair for three days!' Then more and more mothers started to appear, all chattering and nattering over each other.

'What's going on here?' Vibke Paulsen, prim and proper in her starched apron, was in the doorway of the washroom, her hands on her hips.

'Jacqueline is always first into the bathroom and then she takes hours to shower,' Bruno's mother complained, pulling distractedly at her wretched perm. 'But I absolutely must wash my hair.'

'There are three showers,' said Vibke Paulsen. 'So what's the problem?'

'One of them is leaking, and the drain is blocked in the other one,' said the scrawny one, whom the others called Earth Mother, though her name was Liebgard.

'No wonder, if you keep filling it up with sand,' commented the short fat one, whose name was Christa, though nobody ever called her anything but Clingy Mum.

'Full of sand?' asked Vibke Paulsen in astonishment.

'I mixed a scrub made of sand and bran,' said Earth Mother. 'I can't tolerate these perfumed shower gels.'

A storm of indignation broke out among the mothers.

'Typical!'

'Her and her special sausages!'

'What about my sausages?' said Earth Mother crossly. 'I'm a vegetarian.'

Vibke Paulsen raised her arms in a conciliatory gesture. 'Sort it out between you. There's half an hour to breakfast, and I expect to see every one of you there, washed and dressed.'

Meals were taken in the former factory. Sven-Ole had put boards over the conveyor belts and Vibke Paulsen had covered them with white tablecloths. If the high windows with reinforced glass were not so dirty and the walls were not so bare and grey, you might almost think you were in an English boarding school.

At breakfast, they all tried to make a decent impression, because Wohlfarth could see the whole factory floor from the window in his office, and he immediately noticed if one of the pupils misbehaved.

Now, for example, Clingy Mum was nicking a slice of sausage from her neighbour while she wasn't looking. Vibke Paulsen and two mothers who were on kitchen duty were running around between the rows, pouring out tea and coffee. Sven-Ole was doling out rolls.

'So, which is better,' he was asking Jacqueline, known to the mothers as Fitness Mother, 'three four-seed rolls or four three-seed rolls?'

Everyone laughed except Jacqueline, who, because of the piercing in her tongue, couldn't eat any rolls with seeds in them at all.

'Have you done your storytelling homework?' Sophie's mother asked her neighbour, Clingy Mum. 'I just couldn't think of anything.'

'I could,' she replied proudly. 'I wrote an absolutely lovely story about a boy who loves his mother so much that he never leaves her. I'll definitely get an A for it.'

She got an E.

'Do you know how your son would feel if you told him this story?' asked Wohlfarth. This was the only subject he taught. 'He will always have a guilty conscience when he tries to become independent. When I think of my mother ...' Wohlfarth got a faraway look in his eyes, as he always did when he spoke about his mother. 'Ah, when I think of my mother! She made me, she actually *made* me buy my first ice cream all by myself. She put the money into my hand, saying "You'll manage it, son." And I did manage it. You can't imagine how proud I felt afterwards. And so was she.'

Wohlfarth secretly wiped a tear from his eye and cleared his throat. 'Who can tell me what the poet Goethe said once?'

Half a dozen hands shot up.

Sophie's mother, Marie, snapped her fingers. 'I know!' If he asked her now, maybe he wouldn't ask about her homework later.

But Wohlfarth asked Susie, Emily's mother, whose nickname was Snivelling Susie.

'Goethe said we should give small children roots, and older children wings.'

'Very good, Susie. Now I'd like to hear another story. A better one. How about you, Marie?'

Sophie's mother paled. 'I … I couldn't think of anything,' she stammered.

Wohlfarth glanced at the list of names. 'As far as I know, Marie, you have not only a thirteen-year-old daughter, but also a small son. What bedtime stories do you tell him?'

'I read to him …'

'How often?' asked Wohlfarth acidly. 'Every night?'

'Well, I don't always manage to do it every night. In that case, he is allowed to listen to a CD.'

Wohlfarth's face darkened, and Marie quickly added, 'No rubbish, of course. Good children's literature, read by actors, and they cost a pretty penny too. But …'

She broke off in confusion and Wohlfarth wrote something in his notebook.

'It's your turn then, Liebgard.'

Earth Mother stood up and read a horrific story about a little woolly lamb that gets sent to the slaughterhouse.

Sophie's mother commented dryly, 'Any child would definitely drop off to sleep easily after a story like that.'

Wohlfarth banged his fist on the desk. 'Quiet, please!' And to Earth Mother, he said, 'Sit down. F.'

Earth Mother was very disappointed with her grade, and so were most of the others who came in for Wohlfarth's criticism. By the end of class, they were all frustrated.

Everyone except Snivelling Susie. She'd got a B for her homework. It was a rather wacky story about a princess that gets eaten by a dragon who then gets indigestion, and so he spits her out again. And in the end, they fell in love.

'I've never heard such nonsense,' hissed Earth Mother to her neighbour.

Sophie's mother rolled her eyes scornfully.

'A bedtime story doesn't always have to be logical. It's a question of imagination. And – this is very important – there must be a happy ending,' said Wohlfarth.

To everyone's relief, the bell rang. It was much more pleasant to sew dolly clothes or to build a tower of bricks than to be scolded by Wohlfarth.

There was fried flounder for lunch that day, as Hinnerk had had a good catch. There was no need for the manageress of Dune View to marinate it in yoghurt and diet lemonade either, as the so-called trainee models seemed to have healthy appetites. Except Earth Mother, of course, who would eat nothing that had eyes, except potatoes.

After lunch, Wohlfarth came out of his office and down the stairs to the dining area.

'I would like to inform you of a change to the timetable. Unfortunately the workshop "Introduction to Computer Games", led by Herr Kruschke, has had to be postponed. Instead, Sven-Ole will accompany you to the beach and show you how sandcastles are built, since Herr Kruschke is unavailable at the moment.'

Wohlfarth did not mention that Kruschke was having some trouble. One of his Annas had disappeared. At least, she wasn't communicating any more. It might be just a little glitch, or it might be something bigger. Wohlfarth was very annoyed. Everything had gone swimmingly so far, but this he could do without.

The mothers, however, were very pleased. Most of them found computer games boring. And besides, the sun was shining today and it was surely better to be at the sea than to be indoors hunching over a screen. And so, chattering like a flock of birds, they set off in the afternoon with buckets and spades to see who could build the most beautiful sandcastle.

Chapter 11

While Bruno's mother was digging away busily in the sand on this Monday afternoon, screaming when she came upon a dried-up crab, her son was idly clicking the buttons on the remote control. Aunt Anna started to spin, faster and faster, and then she suddenly keeled over. Bruno pressed rewind, and Aunt Anna stood up, stared at him out of extraordinarily glassy eyes and left the room.

She wasn't real! Aunt Anna was a robot! Bruno had only discovered this by accident. On Saturday, his father had presented him with his latest technical gadget: a remote control that you could use to control all the appliances in the house. The electric shutters, the stereo, the digital camera, the television. Bruno's mother was always moaning about all the remotes there were lying all over the house and how you were always sure to pick up the wrong one.

'Your mother will be delighted,' Bruno's father had said. 'It's so simple, even she will be able to use it.'

Bruno wasn't too sure about that. The thing seemed to be complicated enough.

When Bruno's father had headed off on Saturday evening to the local, Bruno had sat down in front of the television and pressed a button. Wouldn't you know it, it was the wrong one. The electric shutters came humming down. When he tried again, loud music came out of the radio. Bruno was starting to get impatient. There was going to be a bantamweight boxing match any minute now on the sports channel. He pressed all the buttons, one after another. At last the TV screen flickered and crackled. Then two men appeared, punching each other on the nose.

Bruno was watching the television with such interest that at first he didn't notice the funny noise. It was a humming kind of sound, and it was getting louder and louder. He turned around irritably. Aunt Anna, who'd been sitting the whole time at the table, flicking through a magazine, had leapt up and begun to spin.

'What are you doing?' asked Bruno.

She didn't answer. She just spun faster and faster.

'Stop!' cried Bruno. 'Please stop.'

Without thinking, he grabbed the remote and pressed one of the buttons. Aunt Anna immediately stopped spinning and stayed quite still. Then she started to speak.

'You don't have to play the piano. You don't have to play the piano. You're allowed to box. You're allowed to bobobobbox, bobobobobobox, bob ...' Her voice was high and squeaky, like when you run a film in fast motion.

Bruno pressed the remote again, and the voice got deep and slow, until it finally came to a halt with a gurgle.

Bruno was by no means a scaredy-cat. He was the only one in his class who was able to watch even the bloodiest scenes in horror films without so much as batting an eyelid. But now he came out in goose pimples and he wished his father were at home. What was wrong with Aunt Anna? Was she crazy, or was she sick? Was there not some awful illness that made you get the wobbles? He'd seen a woman once in a horror movie who was possessed by the devil, and she talked in a distorted voice like that.

'Aunt Anna, what's wrong?' asked Bruno.

But Aunt Anna just stood there with not a budge out of her. Could her strange behaviour have something to do with the remote control? Bruno pressed speculatively on the start button. She stood up, went to the table and started to leaf through her magazine again. Everything seemed perfectly normal. Every evening since she'd arrived, she'd sat at the table looking through a magazine.

'Anna really is a treasure,' Bruno's father had said only yesterday. 'She works like a trooper and doesn't get on your nerves.'

Bruno didn't know much about women. Apart from his mother, the classroom assistant at school and various piano teachers, he hadn't had much experience of them. But all these women had one thing in common: sooner or later, they got on your nerves. But Aunt Anna didn't. That was suspicious. She never accused you of anything. She hadn't even complained when he'd dropped the honey jar at breakfast yesterday, even though it had created the most terrible mess. She'd just bent down with a smile and wiped it all up.

Bruno got up from the sofa and carefully approached the table where Aunt Anna was looking at one of his mother's fashion magazines. His heart was beating wildly. He took the magazine from her and in its place he laid his maths book. Aunt Anna went on leafing blithely through it, nodding every now and again and saying, as she looked at boring exercises, 'Lovely, chic' or 'Far too expensive, I'm afraid'.

Bruno watched her closely. He'd never done that before. Why would he? And now it hit him like a blow: Aunt Anna was a doll! Perfectly made, down to the little birthmark on her upper lip; the glowing, rosy cheeks; the eyelashes. And now he understood why she never ate or drank anything. Until now, he'd thought nothing of it, as long as he'd got something to eat himself.

He touched her speculatively on the arm. It felt smooth. Far too smooth to be skin. She turned to him and said, in her normal voice, 'Hello, Bruno. Are you hungry? Should I stick a pizza in the oven for you?'

'No, thank you,' said Bruno.

Baffled, he went back to the sofa and tried to concentrate on the boxing, but he couldn't. Why was there a doll in his house? To be precise, she wasn't just a doll, but a robot. And what did this all have to do with his mother's absence? Bruno decided to stay up until his father got home and tell him everything. His father would know what to do.

He stood up, said good night to Aunt Anna, who was still flicking gleefully through his maths book, letting out an occasional cry of delight, and took the precaution of locking himself into his room. He waited and waited, but his father must have been very late home.

❋

Bruno's father hadn't surfaced at all on Sunday, and then this morning, he'd left the house very early. That conversation was going to have to wait. But by the time Bruno came home from school, he'd decided not to say anything. He wanted to work out for himself what was going on with this Aunt Anna.

In the meantime, he thought he would tease her a bit. And

that's what he was doing this afternoon. As soon as Aunt Anna had straightened herself out, he asked, 'Where is my mother?'

'She's well, very well, well, well ...'

She never stopped until Bruno pressed the Stop button.

'Where do you come from?'

'Your mother is gone to a health farm on the North Sea. She's well.'

He couldn't get any more out of her, so he went into his father's study and turned on the computer. He entered 'dolls', 'robots' and 'artificial humans' into the search engine and he was astonished to see how far the technology in this field had developed. But this wasn't much good to him. He needed to try some other search term. Just for the fun of it, he typed in, 'Who knows Aunt Anna?'

✳

Emily opened the door to the flat. It was lovely to get home from school without having to be afraid that some catastrophe or other had occurred in her absence. There was no note on the table saying, *I'm in A & E, cut my hand peeling potatoes.* No rubbish bin inside the door to fall over, no burning smell because the iron had been left plugged in for hours. Nothing like that.

When Emily came into the flat these days, there was a nice, clean smell of detergent or a pleasant smell of food. Everything was tidy. It was only now that Emily realised how much she'd hated the constant chaos and how relieved she was not to have to be always worrying about her mother. She didn't have to do that now – or did she?

After the first postcard, a second one had come with almost

exactly the same message, and this one was also unusually neatly written. Emily had finally decided that it was a good sign. Her mother was relaxed, rested, and that showed in her handwriting.

As usual, the table was laid today. Emily sniffed. They were having tuna pizza from the Italian place across the road. She loved tuna pizza, but this was the fourth time they'd had it now. Emily found herself longing for her mother's overcooked pasta.

There were two place settings but Aunt Anna never took more than a tiny piece, and she never ate it anyway. She probably didn't like pizza.

'What's your favourite food?' Emily asked her.

'I like everything, as long as there isn't too much of it,' said Aunt Anna, serving Emily her pizza.

If her mother were here, she'd have sprinkled cayenne pepper on it, or poured chilli sauce all over it. Food could never be spicy enough for her mother.

'Did Mum always like spicy food?' asked Emily.

'She loves spicy food,' said Aunt Anna, nodding.

'Yes, I know that. I'm asking you if she always did, when you were at school together.'

Aunt Anna had told Emily that she had been to school with her mother, and that they'd met again by chance in town a few weeks ago. Emily wasn't surprised that her mother hadn't mentioned this meeting, because she forgot pretty well everything.

'And was she always so …' Emily was looking for the right word. 'So chaotic?'

'Chaotic,' said Aunt Anna. 'Your mother is dreadfully chaotic. Everything she does goes wrong.'

'And was she always like that?' Emily asked.

'Yes, she was always like that,' said Aunt Anna.

Then she stood up, scraped her untouched plate into the bin and put it in the dishwasher.

'I've gone off pizza,' said Emily.

Aunt Anna looked at her.

'Tuna pizza is your favourite food,' she said.

'Yes, but we never have anything else. Could you not cook a proper meal?'

'Like what?' asked Aunt Anna.

'Tinned ravioli, for example,' said Emily. 'Mum often does that.'

'I don't know how to do that. You'll have to show me.'

Emily thought this was a great joke and she laughed. Aunt Anna laughed too, her eyes bright with pleasure.

'I've ironed your blouse,' she said.

'The white one?' asked Emily. 'The one with the ruffles?'

It had been a present from her father to replace the one her mother had ruined.

'Dry-clean only,' her mother had said, reading the label. 'Well that's just great. Now I have to pay for that too. What is your father thinking of?'

And now here was Aunt Anna, holding out the blouse to her. It looked almost better than before. The ruffles billowed at the neck, the lacy bits on the sleeve were lightly starched and brilliant white. Nothing was hanging loose or had gone brownish from a too-hot iron. Emily put out her arms in delight.

'Thank you,' she said, 'thank you very much. My mother would never have done that for me.'

❈

Kruschke was sitting at his computer screens. While the mothers were on the beach learning how to build sandcastles, how to channel the water with wooden dams and how to make bizarre grottos out of egg boxes, he was zapping from one camera to the next, looking at what his Annas were also looking at: children slumped happily in front of the television, stuffing themselves with crisps and chocolate, getting crumbs all over the furniture. He could see that his Annas hoovered, wiped things clean, smoothed out bed sheets and he was very pleased.

Anna 08, who was looking after two boys in Earth Mother's house, was back in communication. It was just that the boys had put cucumber slices on her eyelids. Their mother did that, apparently, and it was supposed to be good for you. Anyway, it didn't do Anna 08 any harm.

But Kruschke had decided, all the same, to monitor his creations more closely. He would be quite happy if that meant he'd have to give up his workshop. In any case, it was as pointless to try to teach women anything about computers as it would be to try to teach a cow to dance on a milking pail. How long was it going to take Wohlfarth to realise that these women were hopeless cases? They were dreadful, and they would remain dreadful.

His Annas, however, were perfect. Yes, he needed to build in a few little improvements, but they were just teething problems. When he saw a constantly spinning image on one of his screens, he wrote a note to himself: *Adjust dance mode*. He had programmed in a few standard dances, just in case. Waltzes were all very well, but what Anna 07 had been doing over the last few days looked a bit dangerous. A module might overheat and important sensors could fail.

Who was Anna 07 with anyway? Oh, yes, Bruno, the would-be boxer. Maybe he was trying to use his Anna as a sparring partner? Kruschke peered more closely. There was the boy. He wasn't wearing boxing gloves, though … And now the camera was turning all by itself, and Kruschke could see a wardrobe flying by, and the sofa, the television. The boy was definitely holding something in his hand. But what was it? The image was spinning faster and faster, and suddenly it went black. Anna 07 must have closed her eyes while dancing. Kruschke was very proud of himself for building in this life-like function.

He zapped again and this time he saw a small boy who was shouting something, his face red with rage. Anna 13 was approaching him, and he was backing off with terror in his eyes. Was that not Sophie's little brother? She hadn't been lying, then, in her questionnaire. He was a right pain in the neck. Now he was just dropping a glass of milk that he had in his hand, and then he ran to the door. And now here came Sophie, who pulled him out of the kitchen and shut the door. The next thing Kruschke saw were the perfectly formed hands of his Anna holding a cloth under a tap. Well, he hoped Sophie would give her little brother a smack on the bottom.

He'd just check to see if the mothers on the beach were getting up to any mischief. Kruschke zapped to a camera whose existence was unknown to everyone but himself. It was in a model aeroplane which swooped through the air, camouflaged as a harmless toy. It was just as well that he couldn't hear the endless nagging and screeching of the mothers – of course, they were fighting again. Earth Mother was just shaking a bucketful of slithery seaweed all over Clingy Mum's feet.

The flying camera had a range of only a few hundred metres,

but that was enough to see that one mother was going away from her sandcastle, all the time looking around her anxiously, and then she went running towards the fence. He knew her immediately by her red hair: Emily's mother. Who else? This woman caused nothing but trouble. While all the other mothers were busily building their sandcastles, she was actually trying to sneak away.

Well, my dear, thought Kruschke, watching how Susie came to a halt in front of the fence, *you won't get very far.* The end of the fence was in the water. It would not be possible to get around it without getting wet for several hours yet, at low tide. But Snivelling Susie very likely didn't know that. None of these women knew anything about tides. Which was just as well.

Snivelling Susie dropped her shoulders, resigned, and trotted back to the others. He'd have to keep an eye on this one. Not only was she the worst student of all, but now it seemed that she was trying to leg it. Of course, it wouldn't be easy to escape from the island. Even if she managed to get away from the area around the factory, she wouldn't get far. There was only one boat a day to the mainland.

But he'd have to watch her all the same. She could, after all, let the cat out of the bag to the inhabitants, that WIMI wasn't a school for models at all, but a school for mothers. There were enough rumours already. It had started with the food. The amounts that the Lührsens were asked to deliver every day didn't square up with a model school. Kruschke gave a soft snort. What a waste of money! Wohlfarth would have been better off investing it in the development and production of Kruschke's dolls. He was almost at the stage where they could go into full production with them.

And not only ones like Anna. He had at least four different models in mind. Then husbands could just order them from the catalogue to be their wives or mothers for their children. Some people would prefer the motherly models; others something a bit more sporty. And, at an extra cost, there would be mothers with special talents. Ones that could stand on their heads or play the harp or knot carpets. In time and with luck he would be able to achieve something that no inventor of artificial humans before him had ever managed: he would produce a doll with feelings. Not one that could laugh or cry at the press of a button, but a doll with a soul. But this much was clear: she would belong only to him.

❋

Susie was standing by her sandcastle. A wave was just lapping around the edges and was knocking it down. A second wave tore another piece away and before long there was nothing left of the castle but little damp piles of sand. Irresolutely, she picked up the spade but then she dropped it again. There was nothing left to save. The other mothers were good at digging and they smoothed the surrounding walls with damp hands. One was decorating her sandcastle with shells. She was writing a message: *For my dearest lo…*

Sven-Ole had bent over to pick up a piece of wood. Nobody was taking any notice of Susie. It was a good opportunity.

I want to go home, thought Emily's mother. *I want to get away from here*. But she could get no further than the fence. She would have to try it from the landward side. She ran quickly to the dunes and scrambled up one of them. Marram grass cut her hands and loose sand slipped under her feet. She glanced back at the beach, but nobody seemed to have noticed that she had disappeared, they were all so busy with their castles. Just another little bit and she would have clambered up the dune and once she'd got over it, nobody would be able to see her any more. At last! Susie wiped her hands on her trousers.

'Well, well! Finished your sandcastle already?' intoned a voice. Susie got a fright but breathed a sigh of relief when she saw Kruschke's head appearing from behind a dune. He didn't look too appealing, with his squint, but he was harmless enough.

He struggled towards her through the dunes. 'What are you doing here?'

'Call of nature,' said Susie with a grin.

'You're not allowed to go to the toilet during class time. That's what breaks are for,' replied Kruschke, wiping the sweat off his brow.

'But I just have to go,' she cried, and in fact it was true.

'In that case, I will accompany you to the school,' said Kruschke. 'Come with me.'

I wouldn't have got very far anyway, Susie thought, as she followed Kruschke. As soon as you climbed one dune, another appeared from behind it. And now the factory could be seen. From here, the barred windows on the ground floor looked very threatening. She was suddenly afraid.

'I want to go home,' said Susie, coming to a standstill. 'You can't keep me here.'

Kruschke turned to face her. 'No problem. However, there isn't another ship today. You'll have to wait till tomorrow. We'll go and see the boss and you can tell him yourself.'

Susie breathed a sigh of relief. She hadn't thought it would be so easy.

Wohlfarth did not seem surprised to see her. On the table in front of him lay a folder with the name Emily on it. On a screen behind him, the motto 'Make your child happy and you save the world' glowed in bright red letters.

'What's this about, Kruschke?' asked Wohlfarth.

'Snivelling Susie wants to leave. She wants to go home.'

'To my daughter,' said Susie stoutly. 'I'm sure she misses me. And I miss her.'

'Right; you miss each other. Well, let's see then. Have you got the DVD, Kruschke?'

Kruschke slid a disc into a DVD player and picked up a remote control. The motto disappeared from the screen, and in its place came a wavering image. A girl with a pageboy hairstyle appeared. At first, the face looked irritated, but then she smiled and stretched out her arms.

'Emmykins! What have you …' cried Susie, but then she clapped her hand over her mouth as Wohlfarth gestured to her to be quiet.

The girl was taking a white blouse from someone. A perfectly ironed blouse with red heart-shaped buttons and ruffles at the neck and sleeves. She held the blouse up to her body and beamed.

Susie knew this blouse only too well. Emily had got it as a present from her father. Impractical to the power of ten! It would take hours to iron all those ruffles and pleats. Which is why Susie hadn't ever done it.

Emily's mouth opened. You couldn't hear what she was saying, but Susie read her lips: 'Thank you. Thank you very much. My mother would never have done that for me.'

Kruschke pressed the remote control. The screen went blank and then the fiery red letters appeared again

'Well, Susie. What have you got to say to that?' asked Wohlfarth in a friendly voice.

Emily's mother said nothing.

'Do you really think your daughter is missing you?' Wohlfarth's tone had got sharper. 'The daughter that wrote this about you …' He started rooting in the folder.

'No, please don't,' whispered Susie. 'Don't read it out.'

'Here we are,' said Wohlfarth, raising his voice. 'Now, listen to this. She writes, "My mother is always getting into scrapes. And then she gets into a bad mood because of it. I do a lot of things for myself. I go shopping, I cook my own food, hang up the clothes. Sometimes she gets these mad ideas. She wakes me up in the middle of the night because she has finally managed to make sushi. But I want to sleep, and anyway I don't like raw fish. I wish she could just be normal. I wish she'd wash my things at the right temperature, iron the blouse that Dad gave me.""

Wohlfarth broke off. 'Do you still want to go home? To go back as the dreadful mother you were before you got here? Or would you prefer to stay here and learn how to make your child happy?' He pointed at the screen.

'Make your child happy and you save the world,' Susie read out tonelessly.

Wohlfarth leafed through the folder again.

'Unfortunately, your grades do not look good. In handicrafts, you've got an E. In all the other subjects, you've just scraped a D.' He shook his head. 'If you go on like this, you'll have to repeat.'

'What do you mean, repeat?' asked Susie in dismay.

'You'll find out soon enough,' said Wohlfarth, closing the folder.

Chapter 12

The atmosphere that evening was almost festive in Wohlfarth's Institute for Mother Improvement. All the students had got good grades in sandcastle building – except, of course, Snivelling Susie – and the sea air did the rest. The mothers helped themselves with great gusto at supper.

'Hey, you've already had two helpings of gherkins and I haven't even had one yet.'

'So? I didn't notice you leaving much of the ham for anyone else.'

'I thought you didn't want any.'

'That isn't the point. It's the principle of the thing.'

Susie took no part in these exchanges. She sat slightly apart, crumbling a piece of bread. She kept seeing Emily's face, the way she had beamed into the camera. Funny that the childminder had filmed the scene, but presumably it had been done to show how much better Emily was doing without her mother.

Susie sighed out loud and was rewarded with withering looks from the others.

'Have you heard? She tried to escape!' Bruno's mother whispered to Sophie's mother.

'I just can't understand it,' said she. 'I have to say, I'm delighted that someone else is having to look after my two fighting brats for a change.'

The suspicious mother with the pointy nose leant across the table and said, 'I'd love to know what kind of mischief my daughter is getting up to right now.'

'Ellen, Marie, Katherine, silence at table. Mr Wohlfarth is about to read something aloud.'

'Oh God, not more out of his diary,' whispered Sophie's mother. 'I can't stand that drivel.'

Bruno's mother nodded in agreement.

Wohlfarth took no notice of these rumblings. He stood up and cleared his throat.

'This entry is from 23 June,' he said, and began to read. 'It was very hot today, and we were sent home early because of the temperature. As soon as I came home from school, I went out into the garden. Someone had filled the old zinc bath with water in the morning, and by now it had got lovely and warm. So, into the tub with me. Peter from next door climbed over the fence. We splashed each other and we played the sinking of the *Titanic*, and in the end we both toppled over, bath-tub and all. Mummy brought towels, then, and rubbed us dry. Then we were allowed to sit in the swinging seat, and she brought us home-made lemonade and freshly baked waffles. Peter was afraid, because he'd torn his trousers when he climbed the fence. Mummy comforted him and darned it so well that you'd need a magnifying glass to see the tear.'

Sophie's mother rolled her eyes and Bruno's mother winked at her.

'Must have been a right supermum.'

'Pssst!' hissed Ramona Bottle crossly, before turning back to look at Wohlfarth. She hung on every word that came out of his mouth.

The poor thing is in love with him, thought Susie. *And he doesn't even realise it.*

'And that evening, I went to bed tired but happy. Mum said my night prayers with me, and told me how much she loves me. "I love you too Mummy," I s –'

Wohlfarth broke off and wiped his eyes.

Clingy Mum was sobbing out loud. 'That's what my Timmy says to me. I miss him so much.'

'Just think, Christa, how much more your Timmy will love you when you have graduated from WIMI,' said Wohlfarth. 'And in case you are wondering how you are doing, I have an interim report here.'

Ramona Bottle passed him a list. He began with Sophie's mother.

'Marie, you are doing well in subjects that have to do with small children. You are the best at building sandcastles and singing lullabies. However, your performance in "Musical tastes of thirteen- to fifteen-year-olds" leaves a lot to be desired.'

'I can't tell one of these bands from another,' said Sophie's mother sheepishly. 'The music is always the same: loud and tuneless.'

'With that kind of attitude, you won't make much progress,' said Wohlfarth and turned to Bruno's mother. 'And as for you, Katherine, you have made a good job of learning the rules of boxing. Your son will be delighted. And even Christa has learnt from the course "Letting go made easy" that you can't mother your child for ever, but there is still plenty of room for improvement. Liebgard gets a special commendation. For the first time in her life, she has cooked a sausage that was not made of tofu.'

Earth Mother smiled proudly.

Wohlfarth went on recounting who had done especially well in what. Then his expression became serious. 'But now we come to something that is not so nice.'

Everyone turned to look at Emily's mother.

'Susie, I haven't a good word to say about you today.'

'Is she going to be thrown out?' asked Sophie's mother, her eyes shining.

'This is not reality TV,' insisted Wohlfarth. 'Having brought you all here, I have taken on a certain responsibility. Nobody will leave this school without a WIMI certificate.'

A hand went up. 'What exactly does that mean?'

'Well, the certificate confirms that you have attended the school. There are three levels of certification. The lowest is "completed", the next is "successfully completed" and the crowning glory would be if some of you left the school with "completed with flying colours".'

'Completed will do me. Nobody asks afterwards if you got good or very good,' said Earth Mother.

'I think we should aim a bit higher than that. Otherwise, the whole thing won't do us any good,' said Sophie's mother haughtily.

'But suppose someone fails?' asked Clingy Mum.

'If anyone does not pass the exam, she will have to stay on and take the course again.'

'No!' shouted Susie, her eyes wide with horror. 'Please don't make me. I couldn't bear it.'

❄

Sophie sat on Nicholas's bed.

'Shall I read you the story of Jemima Puddle-Duck again?' she asked.

Nicholas shook his head. The tears kept streaming down his face.

'Or maybe *The Tale of Little Pig Robinson*?'

More head-shaking.

Sophie couldn't think what to do next. Beatrix Potter's stories had always been a kind of secret weapon to use when Nicholas was sick or distressed. If they didn't help, what was to be done?

The worst thing was that he would hardly speak any more. For the first few days he'd roared, 'Where's Mama? When is she coming home? I want my mama!' But now he just wept quietly.

'It'll all be fine,' George had said that morning as he said goodbye to them. He was flying to Hawaii for a week to introduce a new medication that helped prevent hair loss in older women to a group of doctors who specialised in women's health. 'Anna will look after you well, I'm quite sure.'

It was true that Aunt Anna looked after them. She cleaned and did the washing and the fridge was always full. Since the unfortunate business with the cat food, she hadn't made any more mistakes. All the same, it was hard to feel close to her. Sophie had tried to draw her out with conversation. She asked her which bands she liked, whether she had a boyfriend, where she went on holidays.

'My favourite song is "Yesterday" by the Beatles. I have no boyfriend at the moment. I'm waiting for Mr Right to come along. He has to have brown hair. I like brown hair. I like to go to the seaside on my holidays. But the mountains are also nice. You can go walking. Walking is very healthy. Do you like hill-walking?' Aunt Anna had replied, and somehow it sounded as if she'd learnt it off by heart.

Sophie shut the book.

'Well, then, sleep tight.'

She was just about to stroke Nicholas on the cheek, but he turned away and hid his face in the pillow.

'Good night,' said Sophie softly and turned off the light.

She felt sorry for the poor little fellow. She surprised herself, how quickly her anger at him had disappeared. She went into the living room. There was a whole evening of comedy on one of the pay channels that her mother was so opposed to. She was planning a cosy evening with a packet of crisps. Everything really was much easier when her mother wasn't there. It was a pity that Nicholas didn't see it that way, but then he was only little.

Sophie turned the television on. Her favourite comedian was telling really nasty blonde jokes. Fabulous! Sophie shook with laughter.

'Come here, Aunt Anna, you have to hear this,' she called. Too late, she remembered that Aunt Anna was herself a blonde.

But Aunt Anna also found the jokes funny. Every time Sophie laughed, she laughed too.

'Oh, it's so funny. I've never laughed so much.'

Sophie stopped laughing. Aunt Anna's reaction came across as false, somehow, but maybe she was just trying to be nice. Her mother had always just pulled a face and said, 'I'm sorry, but that's just too vulgar for me.' If she could see her daughter now, chomping crisps in front of the television, she'd probably have a heart attack.

The very thought made Sophie burst out laughing. Aunt Anna followed suit. There was a commercial break on the television. An ad for sanitary products was on, and it was anything but funny. Sophie laughed louder and Aunt Anna laughed too. This was just not normal. Aunt Anna was bending forward, just like Sophie, as if she had a stitch from laughing. Her hair fell forward over her face, revealing the nape of her neck. What was that horrible scar? Sophie looked more closely. It wasn't a scar. It was …

Aunt Anna raised her head and looked at Sophie. Sophie looked her right in the eye for the first time. They were a lovely shade of china blue, with a black ring around the iris.

'I'm going to bed,' said Sophie.

She stood up, turned off the television and scrunched up the empty crisp bag. She felt a bit sick. She didn't know whether it was the crisps that had done it or something else.

'Good night,' said Aunt Anna. 'I'm going to sleep too.'

Aunt Anna slept in Sophie's mother's room. Sophie's mother and George had separate rooms because he often came home very late at night from his travels and he didn't want to disturb her. But Sophie suspected that the real reason was that he didn't want to sleep with her because Nicholas was always cuddled up with her. That was why he was so thrilled that, ever since Aunt Anna had come, Nicholas had started sleeping in his own room.

Sophie couldn't sleep. She kept seeing this extraordinary mark on Aunt Anna's neck. It reminded her of something – but what could it be?

At some point she nodded off and had a terrible nightmare. A giant baby doll in a pink Babygro came crawling towards her, stared at her and opened her toothless mouth. The mouth grew bigger and bigger, a huge black maw towards which Sophie felt herself being drawn, as if by magic. Before she disappeared into it, she woke up, her heart thumping. She knew now what the mark reminded her of.

She hadn't slept long. She could see on the alarm clock that it was just after ten. Sophie turned on the light and got out of bed. She got her chair and pushed it over to the wardrobe. Then she stood up on it and hauled down a box of her old toys. There it was: the doll Sophie had got from her mother on her seventh birthday.

Her mother had been pregnant at the time, and the doll was supposed to be some sort of consolation. But this doll couldn't console anyone. It was too gruesome for that. It looked spookily like a real baby. If you took its left hand, its eyes shone. If you took its right hand, it said 'Mama!' It wet its nappy and then started to grizzle. If you tickled it on the tummy, it giggled. If Sophie's mother thought that this was a way to prepare her for what it would be like to have a baby in the house, she must have been disappointed. Sophie had treated the baby doll extremely badly. She had put all its clothes on her teddy.

Sophie lifted the doll out of the box now. Its skin, which was supposed to be lifelike but always felt a bit slithery to the touch, had gone grey with dust. She turned the doll over. Under the doll's hair two Ws were stamped on its neck. Exactly the same mark that Aunt Anna had on *her* neck. A terrible suspicion was starting to sprout in Sophie's mind. But it wasn't possible – or was it?

Her bedroom door was being slowly opened. Terrified, Sophie pressed the doll to her body. Nicholas tiptoed into the room.

'Can't sleep, Sofa.'

Sophie put the baby doll back in the box.

'She looks spooky,' said Nicholas. 'Like Aunt Anna.'

'Get into my bed,' said Sophie, putting the box back on top of the wardrobe.

She sat down at the desk and fished out her laptop.

'Just have to do a quick search for something.'

It took longer than she'd thought. As she turned the computer off, late in the night, she'd calmed down. She found it comforting to know that she wasn't the only person experiencing the phenomenon that was Aunt Anna.

Chapter 13

'Dad, there's a problem about the school trip,' said Bruno to his father the next morning.

'Could I have another cup of coffee, please, Anna?' said Bruno's father from behind the newspaper, pushing his coffee cup towards her.

'Did you hear what I said, Dad?'

Bruno touched his father on the arm, and Aunt Anna calmly poured coffee right past the cup and onto the floor.

Bruno's father jumped up. 'What an awful mess!' he shouted.

'Me-mess! An awful mess. I'll clean it up straight away, no prob-prob-prob, no problem.' Aunt Anna was already flapping around with a dishcloth.

'I'm talking about the school trip, Dad,' said Bruno again.

At last his father looked at him and said, 'This is the first I've heard of a school trip.'

'Mum signed the form but it hasn't been paid for yet. My teacher is pretty cross about it.'

'And when is it happening?'

'Today.'

His father lowered the paper.

'Today?' he asked, taken aback.

'We're meeting at the train station at ten o'clock.'

'Your mother must have forgotten to tell me about it,' said his father.

'We're going to an island in the North Sea. We're going by train, and then we get a ferry. I need ...' Bruno tried to work out what a trip like this would be likely to cost. 'A hundred euro.'

'Fine, fine. And how long are you going to be staying there?' Dad was taking his wallet out of his pocket.

'Five days,' said Bruno quickly. He would probably be back before that, but then he could say where he'd really been.

'And who is going to do your packing? Not me, I hope.'

'Aunt Anna has packed my suitcase and she will take me.'

'Yes, yes, I'll take take ... take the whole mess mess aw-aw-away,' stuttered Aunt Anna from under the table.

'She'd like to go home then for a while,' said Bruno quickly, 'unless you need her here?'

'No, no, I'll be fine on my own' said his father, not very convincingly.

Good thing his father left everything to do with school up to his mother, thought Bruno. He hadn't been the least bit suspicious.

Bruno sat at his desk and practised his mother's signature once again. It looked a bit wobbly. Not to worry, nobody was going to check it. Then he typed into the computer:

> *Dear Herr Mulke*
> *Bruno is very sick with the measles and won't be at school for a week. As he is very contagious, his school friends may not visit.*
> *Yours sincerely*

That sounded right, Bruno thought. He'd been going to say chicken pox, but then he'd decided that was too harmless. The important thing was to make sure nobody from school came by; otherwise the cat would be out of the bag.

Bruno opened his inbox. The girl he'd come across on the Internet when he had typed 'Who knows Aunt Anna?' and with whom he had exchanged several emails last night had written again:

> *I've checked everything. Your train leaves at 10.35. You have to change in Hamburg. You catch the train for Südersiel on the opposite platform. I'll see you there. You'll know me – I'll have my little brother with me. I can't leave him behind. I'm afraid I couldn't find out on the Internet what time the ferry for Nordfall leaves at.*
>
> *Very excited!*
>
> *Sophie*

Bruno replied:

> *My father swallowed the story about the school trip. That was a great idea of yours. You'll recognise me – I'll have AA with me! Let's hope she doesn't go wild. She's stuttering a lot lately. Obviously something has gone wrong.*
>
> *Till later, then!*
>
> *Bruno*

Bruno had packed his rucksack before breakfast. Now he stuck his toothbrush into the side pocket. Then he thought, had Aunt Anna not had a suitcase with her when she arrived?

He went up to the guest room. The bed was made. A pink nightdress lay neatly folded on the duvet cover. The suitcase was in the corner. It was empty. Aunt Anna's things were hanging in the wardrobe. Bruno stuffed it all into the suitcase. He didn't want anything of hers to remain here.

On the vanity unit lay a hairbrush and a make-up bag. All for show! There wasn't a single hair in the hairbrush, and the make-up bag contained lipstick and eyeshadow that had never been used. He'd like to dump the suitcase and its owner into the rubbish bin. But he couldn't do that. He needed her for the journey. It would look far less suspicious if he were accompanied on the train by his aunt.

He felt a bit queasy when he tried to imagine what awaited them on Nordfall. All he knew, from this Sophie who had written to him in answer to his question 'Who knows Aunt Anna?', was that there was a toy factory belonging to a certain Walther Wohlfarth on the island, and that their Aunt Annas must have come from this factory. But were their mothers also there? And if so, why? Well, this puzzle would soon be solved. Very soon.

❀

Sophie didn't give a thought to how her absence would go down at school. She was going to have to repeat the year anyway. Nobody would be very surprised if she didn't put in an appearance between now and the summer holidays.

She was planning to leave the house just before eight, taking Nicholas with her. She often did that. But instead of going to school, she would go to the railway station, buy a ticket and climb aboard the train for Hamburg. The thought of leaving Aunt Anna all alone in the flat made her feel a bit uneasy. But what harm could she do? At most, she'd clean the place to within an inch of its life.

She opened her schoolbag and put her books on a shelf. Then she filled the schoolbag with a few changes of clothes and her and Nicholas's toothbrushes. Then she wrote a last note to Dragon Monster:

> *Don't be surprised if you don't hear from me for a while. I have to go away. I can't say where. But when I get back, I will tell you the craziest story you have ever heard.*

What she was planning really was crazy. Maybe even dangerous. But then, she wouldn't be on her own. The only thing was, it could be that this Bruno was such a mammy's boy that he wouldn't be able to manage without his mum. Or he might just be plain stupid. You never know with boys.

Lulu came and rubbed against her legs, mewing softly.

'I know what I'll do about you,' said Sophie. 'I'll ask Frau Surbier downstairs to feed you. I don't think I could trust Aunt Anna to look after you!'

❁

Emily came home two hours early from school because sport had been cancelled. Just as Aunt Anna was about to leave the apartment at one thirty to go to the Italian place across the road to pick up a pizza, Emily said, 'No, it's my turn today. I'll cook something nice for us.'

But all she could find in the fridge were yoghurt, cheese and eggs. They'd been there since before her mother had left. But there were enough tins of ravioli in the larder to see them through a siege. Emily opened a tin and heated up the contents in a saucepan.

Of course Aunt Anna didn't eat anything. 'I was in the café earlier and had a piece of chocolate gateau,' she said. 'And I'm so full.'

She always said that. Sometimes it was cheesecake, sometimes apple pie.

The taste of the overcooked ravioli made Emily think of her mother. Which brought a lump to her throat.

She ate up quickly and then she went into her room to write a letter to her mother. Nobody could object to that. A letter wouldn't hurt anyone.

Her father had given her notepaper for her birthday. Pale pink with a border of little red hearts. Her mother would certainly find that in bad taste, but she didn't have any other paper.

> *Dear Mum,*
> *I hope you are well. I am great. Aunt Anna is really nice.*
> *She even ironed my white blouse.*

Emily crossed out that last sentence. It might hurt her mother's feelings.

> *Only she can't cook. When are you coming home?*

Emily chewed her pen for a bit, and then she wrote on.

> *I miss you.*
> *Lots of kisses*
> *From Emily*

Emily folded the letter and put it in an envelope, just as pink as the paper. She was about to stick it down when it occurred to her that Aunt Anna might like to add a few words to it.

'I've written a letter to Mum,' said Emily, coming into the kitchen to Aunt Anna. 'Would you like to add something to it?'

111

Aunt Anna pressed the button of the dishwasher and beamed at her.

'I don't write letters,' she said. 'That's old-fashioned.'

'Yes, I know. Everyone sends emails these days – that or text messages – but I can't reach Mum that way.'

'She has no signal.'

'I know. Can you give me her address, please?'

'She's at the North Sea,' said Aunt Anna. 'And she is well.'

'She will be delighted to get a letter from me. Then she will be even better.'

'She is well,' Aunt Anna said again. 'Would you like some chocolate whip for dessert?'

She opened a packet of chocolate Angel Delight and poured it into a bowl.

'No!' said Emily. 'I want to know –'

'Or would you prefer vanilla?' Aunt Anna said, unconcerned, calmly opening a second packet.

'You must have her address,' insisted Emily. 'They must have given you her address in case anything happens.'

'She's on an island in the North Sea, and she has no mobile connection,' said Aunt Anna. She pointed at the two bowls. 'Which would you prefer?'

'I couldn't reach her on her mobile anyway,' replied Emily, 'because she left it behind her. I told you that already.' She was starting to get impatient.

'The brown one is chocolate whip and the yellow one is vanilla,' said Aunt Anna. 'Which one would you like to have?'

Emily could feel anger rising in her, a dreadful anger.

'Please give me her address right now, or I'll call my father.'

That was an empty threat. Her father couldn't come to the

rescue because he was on holiday with his girlfriend. He'd let that drop quite casually when she had phoned him shortly after her mother went away. 'We'll still be going to Majorca, chicken. Just the two of us.' But even if he had been around, she wouldn't have called him. She could just hear his sharp intake of breath if he heard that her mother had upped and left her in the care of a total stranger. Her father not only thought his ex-wife was annoying but also that she was a bad mother.

He'd often asked Emily if she wouldn't prefer to live with him and his new girlfriend. But for one thing, Emily couldn't stand the woman – she put on such a false smile whenever she caught sight of Emily. And for another, she couldn't do that to her mother. Somebody had to look after her.

'I'm going to get my father,' Emily repeated menacingly.

'Your mother is on an island in the North Sea. She is very well,' said Aunt Anna, unmoved. 'Would you prefer chocolate or –'

'To hell with your chocolate whip!' yelled Emily. She picked up the bowl and poured the stuff all over Aunt Anna's head.

❋

While Emily was staring helplessly at Aunt Anna, who was dripping chocolate gunge onto the floor, three children were looking helplessly around Südersiel station. There wasn't a window with a person behind it anywhere to be seen, no one you could ask a question of. There was a ticket machine beside a graffiti-covered bench. There was a notice on the machine: *Out of order.*

'What a hole this is!' said Bruno.

'That's the way to the harbour,' said Sophie, pointing at a battered signpost.

'I'm hungry,' cried Nicholas.

'You had biscuits on the train,' said Sophie. 'That wasn't very long ago.'

'I'm still hungry,' said Nicholas.

'Maybe there'll be some sort of a snack kiosk at the harbour,' said Bruno.

'Should we just leave these here?' asked Sophie, pointing at the two Annas who had got out of the train with them. They really were like two peas in a pod. Except that Sophie's Anna was wearing a green flowery skirt and Bruno's wore a red one and had a suitcase. The ticket collector on the train had nearly fallen over with astonishment. 'Good Lord! Absolutely identical identical twins.'

'We'd better take them with us,' said Bruno. 'Less chance of things going wrong if we have them than if they are just hanging around here.'

He pulled the remote control out of his rucksack and pressed a button. The dolls started to move.

'We'll have to pay full fare for the pair of them on the ferry,' said Sophie. 'That's going to eat a hole in our money.'

Bruno looked in his wallet. 'I have thirty-three euro left,' he said. 'What about you?'

'Only twenty-one. If I'd known she was going to come after me, I'd have brought more money with me.'

'You didn't look too happy when you got out of the train with her in Hamburg,' said Bruno.

'I told her I was only taking Nicholas to the toilet, but apparently she didn't believe me.'

Bruno pressed on his remote control again and the two Annas hopped forward.

'She's probably programmed to follow you everywhere.'

'I thought I'd been very smart about that,' said Sophie, tapping on her schoolbag. 'She's never followed me to school. But Nicholas let the cat out of the bag.'

'I only said we were going to find Mummy,' said Nicholas.

'Exactly,' said Sophie with a sigh.

It was only a few paces to the little harbour. A few boats were bobbing on the waves. Seagulls were circling and screeching over a fishing boat. A few nets were hanging out to dry on the harbour wall. It all looked very sleepy.

A bigger ship, with the name *MS Nordfall* on its hull, was drawn up beside the pier.

'There it is,' cried Sophie. 'That's the ferry for sure.'

But it wasn't due to sail again until the next day, as they could see from a timetable that was hanging beside a locked-up ticket office.

'What'll we do for all that time?' asked Sophie in dismay.

'First we'll buy ourselves a shrimp roll,' said Bruno. 'There's a fish stall over there, and they are open.' They bought two shrimp rolls and, for Nicholas, a fried fish roll. They asked the stallholder if there was any way of getting to Nordfall sooner.

The stallholder shook her head. 'Why would you want to go there anyway? There's nothing to see, except this weird mannequin school.'

'Mannikins?' asked Sophie.

'Oh, they're called models, these days,' said the fish stallholder. 'But it's the same thing. Those two, they come from there.' She pointed at the two Annas who were standing by the ferry dock looking over the water.

'What do you make of that?' Sophie asked Bruno as they

sat chewing their fish lunch on a bench. 'What on earth do our mothers want with a model school? I don't know what yours looks like, but mine is far too old for that sort of thing.'

'Mine is far too fat,' said Bruno.

'My mama is beautiful,' crowed Nicholas, nibbling at his roll.

'Was I the only one who answered your question, "Who knows Aunt Anna?"' asked Sophie.

'No. There was a Nadine, but she thought her Anna was super and she was delighted that her mother had gone off. She had done nothing but snoop around after her. She was really dreadful.'

'A terrible mother,' said Sophie thoughtfully. Then she leapt up and cried, 'I've got it! Did you fill out a questionnaire about the worst mother in the world?'

'Yes,' said Bruno. 'But what's that got to do with anything?'

'I don't know, but we're going to find out. If only we were on that damned island!'

✼

Emily couldn't sleep. After she had thrown the chocolate whip over her, Aunt Anna had disappeared into her room, or rather Emily's' mother's room, and she hadn't come out.

Emily had knocked on the door and called, 'Aunt Anna, I'm sorry.' Not that she really was sorry.

Now what was she going to do? Should she ring her father and tell him the whole story? He had his mobile with him, of course, and he had said before he left that she could get in touch with him any time. He would be able to get Aunt Anna to talk, and he'd find out where Emily's mother was.

But then he'd have proof that Emily would be much better off being brought up by him and his Saskia than by her mother. Emily felt sick even thinking the name Saskia.

Now she was lying awake, wondering what her mother was doing right now. Was she asleep, or was she awake too and thinking of her?

Then she heard, from the next room, the sound of the wardrobe opening. Aunt Anna must be changing. Her blouse was covered in chocolate whip. Emily put her ear to the wall. She heard the rattle of coat hangers and the squeak of a drawer. It didn't sound like changing. It sounded like packing.

Emily leapt out of bed, pulled on her freshly ironed blouse and a skirt and slipped into her sandals. She could hear the sound of the flat door closing. Where could Aunt Anna be going? Maybe to her mother? It could be that her mother hadn't gone away at all but was in hospital and nobody had dared to tell her. She was going to have to follow Aunt Anna.

Emily picked up her purse, stuck it into her heart-shaped shoulder bag and left the flat.

On the street, she looked around. Aunt Anna was standing at the corner. What could she be waiting for? At that moment, a taxi drove by and Aunt Anna raised her arm. The taxi stopped. Emily ran forward. The driver was just about to put his foot on the accelerator when Emily yanked the back door open. 'I'm coming too,' she cried, throwing herself onto the back seat.

'Is that all right, young lady?' the taxi driver asked Aunt Anna, who was sitting next to him, staring straight ahead.

'Please drive me to the North Sea, to Südersiel. There's a ship waiting there to take me to Nordfall.'

Nordfall? Could that be the island where her mother was staying? Emily wondered.

'That's a long way off. That'll cost you a pretty penny.'

Aunt Anna took a note out of her bag.

'Five hundred euro!' said the taxi man in amazement. 'Put your money away, young lady. It won't cost that much.'

He put his foot down and off they went.

Chapter 14

Kruschke leant back happily. It was all going swimmingly. Anna 01 was on her way home. On the monitor, he could see the steady trajectory of her journey and the hazy back lights of the car in front.

Of course, Wohlfarth must never know that he had prematurely set the 'return home' function in one of the dolls. But how could he have left Anna 01 with that Emily? She had actually attacked her! Someone who starts by flinging chocolate whip around can end up doing something much worse.

There was definitely a bit of a spanner in the works today. Anna 15's speech mode had gone wrong. She was with Timmy, the son of Clingy Mum. Kruschke reckoned that Timmy's having taken her with him to the swimming pool and pushed her into the water could have something to do with it.

The lifeguard had rescued Aunt Anna immediately, and had given Timmy a right telling-off. Her adventures in the pool had robbed Aunt Anna of the power of speech. Kruschke had been trying in vain all morning to restore her speech via a remote connection. Oddly enough, nobody was too concerned about it. Timmy was delighted that there was nobody to nag at him, and his father was equally pleased to have a bit of peace.

Then came this business with Anna 01. It had been a difficult decision for Kruschke to make, but his dolls were too valuable to be the target of flying desserts. But now he'd solved this problem. As soon as Anna 01 arrived in Südersiel, he would be there to meet her.

But first, he had to just check up on the other Annas. One by one, he called them up on his monitors. In most cases, the screen remained blank. That was good. It meant the Annas were in sleep mode. But then, on one screen, a second, smaller screen appeared. King Kong was just stepping on a skyscraper with a wriggling blonde in his hands. Someone was watching television, even though it was a school night.

If Kruschke had been looking at monitor 07 and monitor 13 at that moment, he'd have seen something that he definitely wouldn't like, even though it looked really lovely. He would have seen that two of his Annas had their arms around each other and were waltzing around. Not very far away from him, either. Just an hour's boat ride away, in fact. But Kruschke had turned the monitors off by now. He had a boat to catch, and besides, someone was waiting for him.

❋

Bruno pressed the remote control and the two Annas detached themselves from each other.

'That thing is amazing,' Sophie said. 'What else can you make them do?'

'Haven't a clue,' Bruno admitted. 'I'm just experimenting. Once I pressed one of the buttons and she started ironing like mad, only she used the toaster!'

Sophie laughed softly. She was sitting with Bruno on a bench at the ferry dock. In her lap was the sleeping head of Nicholas. *Small children can sleep anywhere*, she thought enviously. She couldn't as much as close her eyes.

Bruno yawned loudly. It had been a long day. They'd walked out to the lighthouse and back and got something more to eat at the fish stall. And when it started to rain, they'd gone to the railway station to see if there was a waiting room there where they might be able to spend the night, but they were out of luck.

When they got back to the harbour, the fish seller had shut up shop and gone home. The children were all alone. Bruno looked at his watch.

'Nearly eleven.'

'It will be ages before the ferry goes. What'll we do all night?'

'Sleep,' said Bruno. 'Lucky it's stopped raining.' He stretched out on his bench and put his rucksack under his head as a pillow.

Sophie tried to move Nicholas a little, but he woke up immediately and murmured sleepily, 'Mama?'

'Go back to sleep,' said Sophie. 'We'll see Mum soon.'

Nicholas closed his eyes, only to open them again as the beam of a car's headlights fell on his face. Bruno sat up in fright and put his hand over his eyes. Fifty metres away, a taxi came to a halt, leaving its engine running. A woman got out and came towards them. The taxi turned around with a squeal of tyres and drove off.

The woman came closer. At first, they couldn't make her out in the darkness, but when she went past them to the two Annas sitting on the harbour wall, Sophie said, 'Oh my God, it's another one!'

'Hello,' said a little voice behind them. Bruno and Sophie turned around. It was a dark-haired girl with a pageboy haircut. She was very unsuitably dressed in a ruffled blouse and a lacy skirt.

'My name's Emily. What's yours?'

❀

Kruschke was peering ahead. He'd much rather be tucked up in bed than sailing over the waves in this old tub. He checked his watch. He wouldn't be home before midnight. What a waste of time! And all because of this Emily and her dessert strike!

Salty spray spattered his face. His eye was stinging. The moon was shining and he could see the tree stumps that marked out the ferry channel. In the distance he could see the Südersiel lighthouse. He'd soon be there. Anna 01 would be waiting for him. Then it would be into the boat with her, and after that all he had to do was smuggle her into the factory and put her with the others. Wohlfarth would never notice one doll more or less.

That would all change when Kruschke had completed his work on Sarah. In any case, this trip through the night was a good opportunity to test something out.

'Sarah,' he called down into the cabin. 'Come on up.'

A woman with long brown hair came up the steps and stood next to him.

'Take a look at the moon,' he said to her. 'Well, what do you say?'

Moonlight was streaming over the black, black sea like liquid silver. Sarah stood and looked. She looked, as if she wanted to keep this image in her heart for all eternity. Kruschke's fingers were damp with anticipation. How would she react?

'The moon is the only natural satellite of the earth. It orbits it in twenty-seven days, seven hours and forty-three point seven minutes. Its axis is …'

'Yes, yes, that'll do,' Kruschke interrupted her, disappointed.

Sarah had been his first model, and when he had programmed her, he had fed her encyclopaedic information as a way of saving time. He'd only wanted to be able to test if speech mode would work at all. Now he was trying the whole time to reprogram her. He had to make her not only express emotions but actually feel them. If he could achieve that, he would be a greater genius than Einstein.

'Believe me, Sarah, one day Einstein will look like a dunce in comparison to me.'

'Albert Einstein is the inventor of the theory of relativity. The formula goes like this …' Sarah was really cranking it out now.

'Ssshhh!' Kruschke put a hand over her mouth. 'We're nearly there. Go back down into the cabin.'

The day he'd found Sarah sitting in the dunes had been the best day of his life. The swim in the North Sea hadn't done her any harm. All her functions were intact. He was so proud of her. It was such a pain that he had to keep her under wraps. 'But not for long, I promise you that,' he told her.

He was getting closer and closer to the lighthouse. It was lighting up the boat at regular intervals. Kruschke could make out the pier alongside which the ferry was berthed, its white prow gleaming in the moonlight. And someone was standing on the dock. Anna 01, of course.

Kruschke screwed up his eye. Was he seeing double? No, he was seeing triple! There were three Annas standing on the pier, waving their arms.

※

'Here comes a boat!' cried Bruno excitedly. 'Maybe it can take us.'

'Wake up, Nicholas. Wake up!' cried Sophie, shaking her little brother.

'Mama?' asked Nicholas.

'Yes, yes, we're going to see Mum,' said Sophie.

'But suppose they're gangsters?' asked Emily. 'Maybe it's the people who kidnapped our mothers.'

'I don't think our mothers were kidnapped,' said Bruno. 'We'd have got a ransom note if they had been. But instead, we got these dolls sent to us. And they're probably quite valuable.'

Emily had by now learnt from Sophie and Bruno that her Aunt Anna was no schoolfriend of her mother's but a robot in human guise. That explained a lot. But not everything.

'I still don't see why anyone would go to the trouble of swapping a mother for a robot,' said Emily

'That's what we hope to find out,' said Bruno.

The sound of the motor got louder. The three children went towards the pier but made sure to stay in darkness. Sophie was carrying Nicholas in her arms. He was still half asleep. They watched as the motorboat made its way towards the pier and finally stopped near the three Annas. A pudgy man wearing a bobble hat was standing on deck, throwing a rope around a mooring post.

'He doesn't look like a gangster,' said Bruno. 'And he seems to be on his own. Let's go!'

The man helped the three Annas aboard, one by one. He was just about to undo the rope again, when Bruno approached the boat.

'Excuse me, where are you taking them?'

'What are you doing here?' asked Kruschke in surprise.

'We're looking for our mothers,' said Bruno, waving at the others, who were coming hesitantly forward. 'And we believe that they are on an island called Nordfall. You're not going there, by any chance?'

Bemused, Kruschke looked from Bruno to Emily and from Emily to Sophie and Nicholas.

'How do you know? I mean, where did you get that idea?'

'Are you going to Nordfall, yes or no?' asked Sophie, putting her schoolbag on board. 'If so, we want to go with you.'

'I have to make a phone call,' Kruschke managed to get out, and he went into the cabin.

'Come on,' said Bruno, climbing aboard.

The children sat down opposite the three Annas.

'You didn't think we'd rumbled you, did you?' Bruno said to them.

The three kept silent and stared vacantly past him.

'That guy probably turned them off,' whispered Sophie.

Nicholas was crying. One Aunt Anna had been too much for him, and now here were three of them!

'They're not real,' Sophie said, trying to calm him down. 'They're dolls. You know, there's, like, a battery inside them.'

Nicholas nuzzled into Sophie's arms and she put her jacket gently around him.

'OK, I'll take you to Nordfall, to the bossman,' said Kruschke, reappearing.

'The boss?' asked Emily, puzzled. It looked like there was a gangster chief after all. She wanted to get off the boat, but Kruschke had already started the engine, and the boat went puttering out to sea.

It was a silent journey. The aunts weren't able to speak, and the children's eyelids kept drooping. All except Bruno. With the first heave of the boat, he had started to feel most unwell. He felt as if his stomach was almost in his throat. Just look at the horizon, he told himself. Only at the horizon, not at the prow of the boat, which was constantly moving up and down. He belched noisily.

'If you must throw up, please be careful where you do it,' said Kruschke.

He was angry. Wohlfarth was going to give him hell. He could have hidden the three Annas from him, but four children? Still, he could hardly throw them overboard.

Within an hour, they had reached Nordfall. The little harbour was dimly lit. Only at Dune View was there a light over the door. All the other houses lay in darkness. The inhabitants of Nordfall were asleep. Nobody noticed the arrival of the little motorboat that Kruschke was just now carefully mooring.

He disappeared briefly into the cabin again. It seemed to Bruno as if he was speaking to someone. He was probably making another phone call.

When Kruschke came out of the cabin, he said nothing. He just signalled to the children to follow him. The three Annas stayed sitting in the boat, their silly smiles pasted across their faces.

Emily turned to look at her Aunt Anna, in whose hair the remains of the chocolate whip were still visible. How could she ever have taken this thing for a living person? She stuck her tongue out at her.

Kruschke went ahead of them, past Dune View, along a road, till they came to a high fence. Then he unbarred a gate and they went up a driveway that led to a big gloomy building. Everything was dark, except that over a big double door a neon sign glowed. Kruschke unlocked the door and they followed him along a passageway. They crossed a big hall full of shelves. The huge windows let in the moonlight, which lit up extraordinary shapes.

Sophie poked Emily in the ribs. 'Look, it's all toys.'

When she was younger, Emily had loved the toy departments in the big department stores, but this looked spooky. She stumbled against a shelf, and a plush monkey started to bash his cymbals together. Kruschke took hold of the monkey and turned his head right round. The monkey said nothing. It was, when all was said and done, only a soft toy. But Emily got an icy feeling down her spine. Kruschke turned to her. One eye was gleaming like glass. He was winking nervously with the other one.

'Don't worry. I'll soon have him right again.' He spread out his arms. 'All this is my work, you may as well know.'

They came to a large hall, with long tables. An iron staircase led up to the only room where a light was on. A little apprehensively, the children followed Kruschke, who was stumping awkwardly up the stairs. He knocked briefly and pushed the door open.

The man behind the desk looked exhausted. As the children came in, he stood up and offered his hand to each of them.

'My name is Walther Wohlfarth,' he said by way of introducing himself. 'I own this place.'

When he tried to shake hands with Nicholas, the boy hid his hand behind his back.

'I want my mama,' he insisted. 'And I want her now!'

Sophie admired her little brother. The little lad had hardly slept, and, apart from a couple of fish rolls and a few dried-up biscuits, he had hardly eaten anything all day, but he was showing no sign of crumbling.

'Please sit down,' said Wohlfarth. 'I believe I owe you an explanation.'

Chapter 15

Emily sat up with a start and banged her head off a metal bar over her bed. 'Ouch!'

Just then, a mop of hair appeared, hanging upside down.

'Wasswrong?'

The head disappeared, and Bruno came climbing down the ladder from the upper bunk. He was wearing striped pyjamas that were way too big for him. Emily was wearing an old-fashioned flannel nightshirt. It scratched horribly. She rubbed her head.

'I was having a nightmare,' she said, 'and I banged my head.'

Something moved in the top bunk at the other side of the room. Sophie pushed back the blanket and announced, 'I slept like a log.'

'No wonder,' said Bruno. 'We were very late going to bed last night.'

The door opened and a roundy woman came in, carrying a tray of cups and bowls.

'Awake at last?' she said. 'I'll just put your breakfast here on the table. You haven't much time. The ferry for Südersiel is going in about an hour. You know where the bathroom is. I've left you some towels.'

Just as she was about to leave the room, Emily said, 'Frau ... eh ... Paulsen?' She was pleased that she'd been able to remember the name. 'Can you tell me how my mother is?'

Vibke Paulsen gave Emily a sympathetic look.

'Your mother is Susie, isn't that right?'

Emily nodded.

'Well, she finds the lessons hard. She's not good at concentrating. She's easily distracted.' Vibke Paulsen shrugged her shoulders. 'They can't all be as good as your mother, Sophie.'

As if on cue, Nicholas, who was in the bunk under Sophie, raised his head and murmured, 'Mama?'

Vibke Paulsen bent down and stroked his hair. 'Your mama works very hard. You will be astonished, when she comes home, at how much she has learnt here.'

'When is she coming home?'

'In two weeks and two days,' said Vibke Paulsen.

'Is that a long time?'

Vibke Paulsen didn't answer. She just poured some drinking chocolate into a mug and gave it to the little boy.

'Will you all be able to manage on your own until then?' she asked.

'My father is at home,' said Bruno. 'He'll just have to do the cleaning and the washing for a change.'

'And what about you two?' Vibke Paulsen asked, looking first at Emily and then at Sophie.

'My parents are separated,' said Emily. 'I'll go to my father. His girlfriend will look after me.'

She didn't let on that her father wasn't at home. She would have to spend the time until her mother came home all alone.

'Nicholas and I will manage,' said Sophie. 'My stepfather will be home at the weekend.'

'So everything's OK then,' said Vibke Paulsen, relieved. 'You don't want Kruschke's dolls – your aunts, I mean – to go home with you?'

'Absolutely not!' cried Bruno and Sophie, and Emily added, 'They're scary.'

'Yeah,' said Nicholas. 'They're not real, you know.'

'Aren't you observant!' said Sophie.

'And I don't like that man with the funny eye either,' said Nicholas. Then he added in a whisper, 'He killed the monkey.'

'He lost his eye in an explosion,' Vibke Paulsen explained. 'In the factory. It used to be a munitions factory back then. They made gunpowder and bullets, that kind of thing.'

'He's weird,' said Emily.

'Ah, no,' said Vibke Paulsen. 'He's a funny old thing, but he's harmless enough. All he cares about are those inventions of his.'

'And what about Wohlfarth?' asked Bruno.

'Walther Wohlfarth is a wonderful man,' said Vibke Paulsen. 'He refused to carry on manufacturing ammunition like his father and his grandfather. Instead, he started producing toys. His father never spoke to him again.'

'And his mother?'

Vibke Paulsen frowned. 'She was dead by then, I think. He loved her very much, I can tell you.'

'Is that why he set up the school for mothers?'

Vibke Paulsen nodded.

'To tell you the truth, I thought at first that it was a mad idea. But you should just see our pupils! They are all so delighted with it. When I think of the children, how thrilled they will be when they get their mothers back and find that they aren't terrible any more …'

Emily helped herself to a croissant. 'I still don't understand why we can't see them.'

'Herr Wohlfarth already explained it to you. Your mothers are at a critical stage. They are learning to throw off old habits and to substitute new, better habits. If they saw you now, this important process would be interrupted.' Vibke Paulsen gave a pleased sigh, like a child who has just recited her party piece without a hitch.

She went to the door and said, 'Sven-Ole will pick you up in a few minutes and take you to the ferry. I have to go to class now.'

'What happens in class?' asked Bruno.

'Today your mothers are learning how to make custard. I thought every mother knew how to do that, but one of them had lumps in it, another one had a disgusting skin on it, and Susie actually made hers with buttermilk!' Vibke Paulsen laughed. 'She really is a hopeless case.'

When she saw Emily's face, though, she added, embarrassed, 'I'm sorry. I didn't mean to upset you.'

Emily grinned. 'That's all right. My mother just can't cook. I know.'

❄

'I have a question for you landlubbers,' said Sven-Ole on the way to the ferry. 'Have you heard the one about the two sailors?'

Emily turned and looked back. Vibke Paulsen's house, where they had spent the night, looked so nice, quite harmless. It wore its thatched roof like a nice warm cap. Roses in colours from soft pink to deep violet were climbing up the wall. The shutters were a fresh and gleaming green. Emily would love to have had a holiday here with her mother. Maybe they would come back here some day, later, when this was all over.

But although everything seemed so peaceful – little white clouds in a blue sky, pretty houses in colourful gardens – Emily could not shake off a certain sense of menace.

The others didn't seem to be bothered. Bruno was laughing at the joke that the nice young man was telling and Sophie seemed not to be so crotchety. Even her little brother had stopped asking for his mama. He was running towards a black and white cat that was sitting outside a garden gate licking itself clean.

'Do you teach in the WIMI too?' asked Bruno.

'Sure I do,' said Sven-Ole proudly. 'I'm teaching football clubs this afternoon. By the way, your mother got an A in boxing, did you know that?'

'My mother? Boxing?' Bruno couldn't believe his ears. 'You must be mixing her up with somebody else. My mother thinks boxing is repulsive.'

'She used to think that,' said Sven-Ole. 'That's what we're trying to do here, see. We're trying to get them to unlearn their old ways.'

The ferry was waiting for them at the dock. Its hull was a gleaming white and the brightly painted chimney belched out cheery clouds of steam.

Swantje, the maid at Dune View, was shaking out tablecloths outside the front door of the guesthouse. Seagulls swooped around her, screaming, hoping to fall in for a few crumbs. The postman was leaning against his van, chatting to Lührsen, the guesthouse owner. When he caught sight of Sven-Ole, he tipped his hat and called out, 'So, how are your models getting on? It's a pity we never get to see them.'

'Models?' Sophie looked quizzically at Sven-Ole.

He rolled his eyes. 'Fish-heads. They haven't a clue.'

Then he said goodbye to the children and watched as they boarded the ferry. When they were standing at the rail that ran around the deck, he waved to them, and then he set off towards the factory.

There was a loud tooting sound, and the boatman pulled in the mooring rope. A woman appeared suddenly from the dunes. She ran towards the ferry, shouting something, but the wind snatched the words out of her mouth. She gesticulated wildly, and suddenly it became clear what she was shouting, 'Stop! Stop!'

The boatman grumbled, but he put the rope back around the mooring post.

It was then that Emily recognised the woman. 'Mum!' she called. 'Mummy!'

She wasn't sure if her mother heard her because, just at that moment, the woman stumbled, lost her footing, and would have fallen if Sven-Ole hadn't got hold of her.

'Let me go!' cried the woman. 'I want to get on the ferry. I want to get away from here!'

Sven-Ole held her fast by the wrist.

A rickety old van came rattling along and stopped beside them. The passenger door opened, and Sven-Ole pushed the woman into the vehicle. The driver turned the van and drove off the way he had come. It all took less than two minutes. Nobody seemed to notice. The ferryman pulled his rope in again.

'Did you see the madwoman?' asked Sophie, shaking her head.

'That madwoman is my mother!' gasped Emily. 'I have to go to her!'

She ran down the gangway to the lower deck. Bruno and Sophie followed her. Only Nicholas remained at the railing, crowing with delight as the seagulls caught pieces of bread he was throwing for them as they flew by.

'Where do you think you're going, girl?' called the ferryman as Emily ran towards the stern. 'You can't disembark now!'

He was right. The ferry had moved away from the pier and had started to sail away.

The children looked at each other.

'Huh!' said Emily. 'They're supposed to be here of their own free will, right? I don't think so. I had this funny feeling when we were in the factory yesterday.'

'Do you really think,' asked Bruno, disbelievingly, 'that they are keeping our mothers here by force? But there are too many of them for that, aren't there?'

'Well,' said Sophie thoughtfully, 'maybe some of them are happy enough to be here. But not Emily's mother, for starters.'

'I have to get to her,' said Emily softly, licking her lips. They tasted salty, either from tears or from the sea-spray. She had to get back to the island. She couldn't go home with this image of her totally distraught mother in her head.

'There's no way the ferry is going to turn around for us,' said Bruno. 'Unfortunately.' The rolling and pitching of the boat was making him sick again.

'Well, then, I'll just have to stay overnight in Südersiel and wait until it goes back in the morning.'

'Have you got money?' asked Bruno.

Emily shook her head. Aunt Anna paid for the taxi yesterday.

She only had enough money to get back home by train.

Sophie pulled out her purse. 'I've got fifteen euro left. That's not enough.'

'For one person, it might be,' said Bruno.

'But not for the four of us,' said Sophie. 'I'm not planning on leaving Emily on her own.'

❋

'Kruschke, you are an idiot!' said Wohlfarth for the third time. 'Not only have your damn dolls completely malfunctioned –'

'Only three of them,' Kruschke managed to interject. 'Three out of seventeen – that's not even a twenty per cent failure rate. It's –'

'It's a catastrophe! Not only have they failed, but they turn up here with those children in tow. Have you any idea what a setback that would have been for my whole project if their mothers had seen them?'

Kruschke was offended. 'But they didn't see them.'

'Yes, but only because I managed to convince the children that we have their mothers' best interests at heart, and, of course, theirs also.'

Wohlfarth cleared his throat. 'What is our motto, Kruschke?'

'Make your child happy and you save the world,' muttered Kruschke, scratching circles on the ground with the toe of his shoe.

'Exactly. It's about making children happy in the long term. That's the only way the planet can survive.' Wohlfarth raised his arm like a preacher in church. 'Happy children mean happy adults; happy adults don't go to war: they live in harmony with each other and with the environment.' Wohlfarth's index finger poked Kruschke in the stomach. 'And what have your Annas done? Not only have they failed to make these children happy, they have gone so far as to make them *afraid*.'

'The only one who's afraid is that spoilt little boy,' said Kruschke.

'Even a spoilt little boy has a right to happiness,' said Wohlfarth. 'That's why the mothers are here. That's why I have invested not only my money but also my time. And you …' Wohlfarth was working himself up into a rage. 'You're cobbling together some sort of loopy puppets that go into a spin when someone uses a remote control or who keep croaking the same old thing, like a parrot.'

'That was a regrettable mistake, but the others, my other robots, are functioning beautifully. I can show you the photos,' said Kruschke eagerly. 'Earth Mother's sons actually want to be adopted by Anna 08!'

'Forget it.' Wohlfarth waved him wearily away. 'We have a much more pressing problem. What are we going to do about Emily's mother?'

'We could send her back,' suggested Kruschke.

'Absolutely no way!' cried Wohlfarth. 'So that she can go around telling everyone how horrible it is here? It is crucial that the mothers are delighted with their experience here. My plan is that, in future, mothers will come here to my mother improvement centre of their own free will. I want them to be tearing their hair out to spend thousands of euro to come here and learn how to become a perfect mother. I'll knock down the factory and build a lovely new school with nice bright rooms.

There'll be single rooms, like in a hotel, a wellness centre and –'

'And what's going to become of my Annas?' asked Kruschke, horror-stricken.

'You and your Annas – bah!' Wohlfarth spat contemptuously. 'Nobody has the slightest interest in your Annas any more.'

Chapter 16

The children were sitting at the harbour eating shrimp rolls, all except Nicholas. As usual, he had one with fried fish fillet, the nearest thing to fish fingers.

Bruno counted the money he had left and gave a worried frown.

'We can't sit around until the morning, waiting for the next ferry,' said Sophie, chewing on her roll. 'We'd go nuts.'

'No,' said Bruno, 'but we can hardly swim it! Though I'd nearly prefer that than to set foot on another boat.'

'I didn't bring my swimsuit,' said Emily.

'Sofa has a bikini,' said Nicholas helpfully, 'but she never wears it because it makes her tummy stick out.'

Bruno laughed and Sophie shouted, 'You miserable skunk!'

Nicholas let his roll fall open and the fillet of fish landed in the muck.

Normally, Nicholas would have started to screech at this point, but instead he just picked up his fish, wiped the sand off it and stuck it back into his bread roll.

'Ugh! He can't eat that!' cried Emily, horrified.

'Oh, for goodness' sake,' said Sophie. 'A spot of sand won't hurt. It'll do his tummy good.'

'How many kids would you think filled out that questionnaire?' asked Bruno.

'Haven't a clue,' said Sophie, 'but I know now why my Aunt Anna tried to feed Nicholas cat food. She hadn't been programmed to cope with a cat. I ticked "none" in the "pets" category.'

'What made you do that?' asked Emily.

Sophie went red. 'I was so cross with my mother, I only filled in mean stuff in the questionnaire. I kind of thought, if I admitted that we had a cat, it would look as if she wasn't so awful after all.'

'I wish my mother would let me have a pet,' said Bruno. 'But she worries so much about the carpets.'

'Do you really think Wohlfarth's school is going to make perfect mothers out of them?' asked Sophie.

'Definitely not out of mine,' said Emily. 'Frau Paulsen says she got detention three times.'

'Cool,' said Bruno.

'I'm being kept back this year for the first time,' said Sophie, 'and it's not a bit cool; it's just stupid.'

'But why?' asked Bruno. 'What's the reason?'

'I didn't do a tap,' admitted Sophie. 'I sort of thought that if my mother saw I was doing badly at school, she might finally take a bit of notice of me – you know, worry about me.'

'But she didn't, right?' said Emily.

'Yeah, she only has eyes for the little fellow. Nicholas this and Nicholas that. That's how it goes, from dawn to dusk.'

'Nicholas this and Nicholas that, Nicholas makes a rat-a-tat-tat!' sang Nicholas, his cheeks bulging with fish and bread.

'He is kind of sweet, though, isn't he?' said Emily.

Sophie spoke softly. 'Yeah, I suppose he is. I've always found him really annoying, but I have to say,' she added more loudly, 'since it's been just the two of us, I've started to see what a smart little lad he is. Aren't you, Nicholas?'

'I'm smart, smart, smart,' crowed Nicholas proudly.

'Then maybe you can tell us how to get back to that island,' suggested Bruno.

Nicholas pointed at a couple of fishing boats bobbing up and down in the harbour. 'On one of those!' he suggested.

Bruno wiped his greasy fingers on his trousers. 'That's not a bad idea,' he said. 'Come on, let's go.'

The children went over to the fishing boats and Bruno read out their names: '*Henrietta Helgoland* and *Seagull III*. That one looks a bit battered. But look at this one: *Swantje, Nordfall*. All we have to do is wait for the fisherman to come back and set sail for the island.'

'Do you think he'd take us?' asked Emily.

'We can always ask,' said Bruno. 'All he can do is say no.'

❁

Hinnerk was more than a little surprised to find four children waiting for him when he got back to his boat.

'Could you possibly take us back with you to Nordfall?' asked Emily. 'It's really urgent, and the ferry isn't going until tomorrow.'

'We haven't got much money, though,' added Sophie.

'Please,' said Bruno.

Hinnerk did sometimes take people over to the island. The vet, for example, if he needed to vaccinate the sheep and had missed the ferry. He'd never taken children, though. But he was in a good mood. He'd had a good catch.

'I only have one life jacket,' he said.

'Nicholas can have it,' said Sophie. 'He can't swim.'

'I can,' said Nicholas. 'But only with water wings.'

'All right, then,' said Hinnerk.

The children sat on upturned boxes that were normally used for carrying fish. You could tell by the smell. Emily wrinkled her nose, and Hinnerk said, 'You can go down into the cabin if you like.'

Bruno shook his head. 'We're fine here.'

'So,' asked Hinnerk, turning the engine on, 'what's this urgent business you have on Nordfall?'

'We're going to see my mama,' said Nicholas.

'Our mothers are in the WIMI,' explained Sophie, watching to see Hinnerk's reaction.

But he looked expressionless. 'Well, I'm sure they'll be delighted to see you.'

'If only Wohlfarth will let us,' said Emily. 'He's a bit weird, isn't he?'

Hinnerk laughed. 'Weird is right. My cousin, Sven-Ole, works for him – he could tell you a thing or two. Especially about that business with his mother. There are pictures of her all over the place. She's supposed to have been the best mother in the world.'

'And was she not?' asked Bruno.

Hinnerk shrugged. 'None of us knew her. She's been dead for ages. In my opinion, everyone is fond of his own mother, isn't he? But the way Wohlfarth goes on about her, it's just not normal.'

Emily's mother was sitting in the common room, chewing on her pen. While the others were at lunch, she had to write out twenty times: *I must not leave the school during class time, because otherwise I will never learn to be a good mother.*

Her fountain pen ran out of ink on the word 'class'. She stuck another cartridge in, but she got it upside down and ink came spurting out all over her copybook. The blue blots mixed with her tears and made a light blue streak.

If only Sven-Ole hadn't caught her, and if Wohlfarth hadn't been passing by just at that moment, she'd have been on her way home by now. On her way to Emily. Tears welled up in her eyes again. She had such a longing to see her daughter that she'd convinced herself she had, in fact, seen her. She'd imagined that Emily was on that ferry and had waved to her. But of course that was impossible. Emily didn't even know she was here.

And even if she did know, how could she have made her way to Nordfall? She was probably thrilled that this troll was at home with her instead of her mother and spent all the time ironing her stupid frilly blouses. Though she did have to admit, Emily always looked so sweet in those things.

Susie lifted her head. The door opened and Vibke Paulsen came into the room.

'Have you finished your lines? You must be hungry. I've wangled you a piece of fish.'

'I wasn't able to write,' said Susie, pointing at the blotted page. 'My pen is broken.'

'Oh, Susie, will you ever learn?'

'I want to,' said Susie, jumping up. 'I want to learn to iron, for Emily. She loves clothes and she has all these blouses with lots of frills and tucks and pleats.'

'So I've noticed,' said Vibke Paulsen with a smile.

'How can you have?' asked Susie, irritated.

'Eh … well, on the videos that Kruschke has shown us,' said Vibke Paulsen. She added quickly, 'Come with me to the sewing room.'

'But what about my lines?' asked Susie.

'We'll think of the ironing as a kind of punishment instead,' said Vibke Paulsen with a sigh.

Susie ironed like a woman possessed. At first, all she did was iron creases into the garments that Vibke Paulsen gave her. She scorched a collar and tore a button off. But the tenth blouse that she ironed was almost perfect, and by the time she got to the fifteenth, the ruffles were rippling along the seams like sails in the wind.

'Snivelling Susie's problem is solved,' said Vibke Paulsen at the daily reporting session in Wohlfarth's office. 'I think she has finally grasped what it's all about here.'

'That's good news,' said Wohlfarth. 'But do you think she can do it again, or is it just a fluke?'

Ramona Bottle and Sven-Ole were riffling through their papers.

'She's stuck on an E in practical theory,' said Ramona Bottle. 'She really needs a B to bring up her average.'

'Well, she's not going to get that kind of mark from me,' said Sven-Ole. 'In my group, she's easily the worst. She just can't seem to get a grip. Never has the right equipment. Yesterday I caught her scrabbling about in the sand with a spoon because she'd mislaid her spade.'

'I don't think it's quite as bad as all that,' said Vibke Paulsen. 'There are always people who pick things up quickly and ones who are late developers. Susie's problem is that she never has her mind on the thing in hand. She's always thinking about something else. When she concentrates, though, she can do it.'

❁

While the other mothers were chattering about their homework, Susie bent over double on her chair.

'What's the matter with you now?' asked Sophie's mother, who was sitting next to her.

'That fish we had at lunchtime – I think it was a bit off,' groaned Susie.

'Rubbish,' said Earth Mother. 'We all ate it, even me. And nobody else is sick.'

'You're just imagining it,' said Sophie's mother bossily.

Snivelling Susie gave a loud belch. Sophie's mother drew back in disgust.

Susie stumbled into the bathroom, her lips pressed together.

'I bet she'll spend the next few hours on the loo,' said Bruno's mother with a smirk. 'Her face was green.'

'Then she won't have her homework done for tomorrow,' said Clingy Mum. 'Again. There'll be trouble, mark my words.'

'Not my problem,' said Earth Mother, putting her arm over her copybook. 'Hey, copy someone else.'

'I wasn't copying.'

'No? So then how come you're always squinting over this direction?'

Squabbling broke out again and everyone forgot all about

Snivelling Susie and the gone-off fish she might have eaten.

Susie was sitting on the loo, chewing thoughtfully on her bottom lip. She was going to have to find some way out of here. There wouldn't be a ferry until tomorrow, but Susie was sure that if she could just get out of the building she'd be able to find someplace where she could spend the night in safety. The day she'd arrived, she'd seen this guesthouse called Dune View. The whole population of the island couldn't be in cahoots with Wohlfarth and Kruschke.

Someone came into the bathroom to wash their hands. She gave a few horrible groans and flushed the loo.

When it had all gone quiet again, she opened the door of the cubicle and slipped out of the bathroom. She scuttled along the corridor, off which were the bedrooms and workrooms. She considered for a moment whether she should take her handbag with her, but it was empty anyway. As soon as they'd arrived, Wohlfarth had confiscated all their keys, wallets and mobiles. 'In case they got stolen.' Susie didn't see how a burglar could possibly get into the building. It was like Fort Knox. But they hadn't taken Porky. She had the lucky pig safely in her pocket.

She entered the big hall. It was always gloomy in here, whether or not the sun was shining outside. A diffused light came through the dirty skylights. There had to be some side entrance, apart from the main factory gate.

Susie squeezed her way between the crowded shelves. Her nose was full of dust. She suppressed a sneeze.

Every time she reached the end of a row of shelves, she came to a dead end. She was just about to give up and go back when she found herself faced with a curtain of thick plastic that you couldn't see through. What could be hiding behind it?

She raised the curtain and slipped under it. It was even darker in here. But she could make out shoes. Several pairs of black high heels. She touched the black leather and wondered what on earth women's shoes were doing in a factory that used to make toys. Then she touched a foot. More than a foot – a leg.

She stood up and found that she was face to face with a woman. A woman with pale hair, her lips open, as if to ask a question, and an empty stare. Then the lips moved: 'Would you like to play with me?' The same sentence was repeated: 'Would you like to play with me?'

But the second time, lots of mouths were saying it. There wasn't just one woman. Susie could see at least ten of them, all repeating the same sentence over and over: 'Would you like to play with me? Would you like to play with me? Would you like to play with me?'

That was when Susie started to scream.

Chapter 17

There is nothing more ridiculous than a grown woman who is scared of a few shop-window mannequins. Susie laughed at herself. But then her throat closed over, and she had to shut her mouth to prevent herself from shouting again. With joy, this time.

It had to be a dream. Here came a girl. A girl she knew only too well. She came out from among the dolls.

'Emily!' cried Susie.

'Hush,' said Emily, putting a finger to her lips. 'Come with me!'

She dragged her mother between the Annas to a narrow door that stood ajar.

It led into a little yard. There were three children there: a chubby girl with wild dark hair; a freckled boy, beaming all over his face; and a little blond lad.

'This is Sophie and her little brother, Nicholas,' said Emily. 'And that's Bruno.'

'I know you. I saw you in the pictures. The ones Kruschke showed us. Your mothers are here too, aren't they?'

Bruno nodded.

'But how come you're here, on the island?' asked Susie. 'And how on earth did you get into this factory?'

'Just as we arrived,' said Bruno, 'a van was coming out, and the whole place was open.'

'That'd be the Dune View van,' said Susie. 'Picking up the leftovers from lunch.'

'So we just wandered in.'

'Looking for our mothers,' Sophie added. 'But there was no-one here.'

'They were all out on the beach,' said Susie, still rather puzzled. 'I was ironing.'

'Ironing?' asked Emily, astonished.

'Then we saw the drinking chocolate woman,' said Nicholas, 'and we hid.'

'Between the Annas,' said Sophie.

'Annas? Do you mean the mannequins?'

'They're not mannequins, Mum,' said Emily. 'They're robots that look like people.'

'They're ssoooo spooky!' breathed Nicholas.

'Then Bruno found the door,' said Emily, 'and we were just going to explore the factory when we heard you calling out.'

'But I still can't work out how you got here in the first place.'

'It's a long story,' said Emily, taking her mother by the arm. 'For now, we need to work out how to get out of here.'

'Without being seen,' added Bruno.

'Maybe the gate in the fence is still open,' suggested Sophie.

They went around the corner of the building. From here they could see the exit and the fence. The gate was not open.

'Now what?' asked Sophie.

Susie checked her watch. 'If our luck holds out, we'll be able to get through to the other side of the fence. I did that myself this morning. The tide was out. Anyone know anything about tides?'

Bruno shrugged. 'We did it in geography, but I wasn't listening.'

'Maybe it'll be OK,' said Susie. 'Let's all go into the dunes.'

'Sophie and Bruno worked out that their mothers were on Nordfall,' said Emily, stumbling through the sand beside her mother. 'And I came here with Aunt Anna. I mean, with one of those dolls that you've seen.'

'That fisherman guy brought us here from Südersiel on his boat,' added Bruno, 'and Wohlfarth lectured us for ages about how great his mother school is and how we mustn't disturb our mothers.'

'We spent the night with Frau Paulsen,' said Emily. 'She was really nice.'

'She made us drinking chocolate,' said Nicholas.

'And then we went back to the mainland on the ferry,' said Emily.

'So I *wasn't* imagining it when I thought I saw you on deck.'

'I saw you too. I saw the way they bundled you into that car.'

'So Emily said we had to rescue you, and that's why we came back,' said Sophie.

'I found the ship,' Nicholas announced proudly.

'Yeah, you did,' said Emily, stroking his hair. 'A fisherman brought us back to Nordfall.'

'How is my mother?' asked Bruno.

'She's fine,' said Susie. 'They're all fine, except me.'

'You can tell us all about it later,' said Emily. 'We won't get away from here before tomorrow.'

'Oh, God, I feel sick,' groaned Bruno, 'when I think about having to get on a boat again.'

'Only this one last time,' Sophie said to comfort him. But she was wrong about that.

They went running down the last dune then and could see the sea glittering in the distance. The six-foot fence cut across the bright sand like a black line to their left.

'Do you not think you'll be missed?' Emily asked her mother as they ran along a wooden pathway to the strand.

'Not before nine. That's when Wohlfarth's story time starts. That's what we call it when he reads out of his diary. They won't take any notice if I'm not at supper. The others think I have stomach cramps and that I've been in the loo the whole time.'

'Get a move on, Nicholas,' called Sophie, as her brother stopped to watch a black beetle scuttling over the sand.

'I can't go any further,' moaned Nicholas. 'You'll have to carry me, Sofa.'

'Come on, I'll give you a piggyback,' said Susie, hunkering down. 'We're nearly there.'

When they reached the beach, they ran along the damp sand towards the fence.

'I want that shell!' screeched Nicholas over Susie's shoulder, pointing at the gleaming mother-of-pearl of an oyster shell. He leant over so far towards it that Susie stumbled and she and Nicholas both went tumbling down onto the sand.

'Typical!' muttered Emily, shaking her head as she helped her mother up. Nicholas got his shell and off they went again.

'Damn!' said Bruno when they reached the fence. 'We're too late.'

Water was swirling around the fence posts in little eddies.

'Or too early,' said Emily's mother. 'Maybe the tide is going out.'

'We'll have to try it,' said Sophie. 'It can't be all that deep.'

She hoisted up her trouser legs and waded into the water. At the end of the fence it reached her knees.

'No problem!' she called to the others. 'Come on.'

Bruno followed her. The water came up to his thighs. 'Eek,' he complained. 'It's cold.'

Next came Susie with Nicholas. She clung onto the fence posts to keep herself from being swept away by the water, which was swirling more strongly now. Nicholas thought it was great fun. He pulled her by the hair and called, 'Hey up, sea horsie. Hey up!'

Emily hung back. She was afraid to go into the water. It looked anything but inviting. Brown bladderwrack and dirty grey foam floated on top of it. Her lovely white skirt would be good for nothing but a dishcloth after this. She looked out over the ocean. The sun was still on the horizon, but there was no more warmth in its rays. Emily came out in goosebumps.

'What are you waiting for, Emily?' called her mother.

'Come on!' called Sophie impatiently.

Emily took her sandals in her hand and yanked her skirt up high. The water was horrible. Cold and sort of slimy. Her foot touched something slithery. Emily gave a yell, lost her balance and fell into the water.

Sophie gave a loud laugh from the other side of the fence. It just looked so funny the way Emily got up, for all the world like some sort of water nymph, teetered around and then plopped into the water. But Sophie soon stopped laughing when she realised that Emily couldn't get up. She was trying to hang on to the fence, but she was being swept away by the water, which was coming from all sides now.

Susie cried out and went back into the water to come to the aid of her daughter. Bruno and Sophie stood transfixed, on dry ground.

'Are they going swimming?' asked Nicholas.

'Do something!' cried Sophie, when she saw how Emily and her mother were being swept further and further away from the shore.

'What *can* we do?' asked Bruno in bewilderment.

Susie was trying to swim towards Emily, but the current was pulling the two of them in opposite directions. Then came the sound of a motor.

'A boat!' exclaimed Bruno, relieved. 'There's a boat coming.'

With her last ounce of strength, Emily reached for the lifebelt that was thrown to her. Her ears were ringing. It had all happened so quickly. One minute she could feel the sandy bottom of the sea under her feet; the next minute she was being whisked away by the water. Her mother was shouting something to her, but the wind carried her words away.

'Hold on!' called a voice. 'I've got you.'

Kruschke! Emily would never have thought she'd be so glad to see this funny little bald creature again.

'My mother is ...' She gasped for air and swallowed a gulp of salt water.

Kruschke pulled her in and helped her onto the boat. She scraped her leg on the side of the boat, but eventually she was in it, lying full length on deck, like a fish that had just been landed.

'Emmykins! My baby! Are you all right?'

'Mum!'

Her mum was bending over her, water streaming from her hair on to Emily's face.

'Never underestimate the tide. It has cost many a person their life,' said Kruschke.

Emily looked at him. This man had saved her life. Her life and her mother's.

She half sat up and looked towards the shore. Bruno and Sophie, holding Nicholas by the hand, were still standing on the same spot on the far side of the fence.

Emily raised her hand to wave but let it drop immediately. She felt weak. Everything was starting to spin. She could feel her mother's hand supporting her head, and then everything went black.

When she opened her eyes again, Kruschke was mooring the boat to a little pier. It was already dusk.

Emily gave her head a careful shake. 'Please take us to the harbour. I want to go home with my mother.'

Kruschke turned to look at her. 'There's no ship at this hour. I'm sure you'll be glad of a nice soft bed for the night.'

Emily looked down at herself. Her lovely white skirt was sticking to her legs like a grey rag. It was ruined.

'Only if my friends are there too.'

'Not to worry, they will be,' said Kruschke, passing her a handkerchief.

'And my mother?' asked Emily.

'It's all sorted,' said Susie. She was all wrapped up in a blanket and Emily couldn't see her expression. 'You're sleeping here tonight and tomorrow you're all going home.'

'But you're not coming with us?' asked Emily, horrified.

Her mother shook her head. 'No, I'm staying until I've finished here.'

'Whenever that may be,' muttered Kruschke.

❀

As the boat disappeared from view, Bruno said, 'We should inform the police.'

'Would you think there's a police station here?' asked Sophie.

'Haven't a clue,' said Bruno, 'but we have to tell someone that Emily and her mother have been kidnapped.'

'Pulled out of the water, you mean,' Sophie corrected him. 'First her mother and then Emily. I don't think you could call that kidnapping. It looked more like Kruschke saved them from drowning.'

'But now they're back in the factory, and they definitely didn't want to go there.'

'You're right,' said Sophie. 'Come on, Nicholas, you'll have to walk a few more steps.'

Nicholas had stuffed his pockets with shells. He pulled a crab out now.

'Look, he's still alive.'

The crab waved his pincers tiredly.

'Don't put that into your pocket!' said Sophie sternly. 'Put it back in the water.'

They trudged through the dunes till they came to a narrow cement path that led into the village. The thatched cottages seemed to be hiding among wild roses behind high hedges. Only at Dune View was the door left invitingly ajar.

The children entered the bar. Lührsen, the guesthouse owner, was standing behind the counter, washing beer glasses. Swantje was wiping down the tables. They were all unoccupied, except one by the door. Hinnerk was sitting there, staring glumly into his empty glass.

'Well, did you visit your mothers?' he asked when he saw the children.

He held out his glass to Swantje. She shook her head, but she went to the bar all the same to pull a new beer. She put the glass in front of the fisherman and then bent down to Nicholas.

'Well, laddie, are you hungry? I think we have some fried fish left.'

Nicholas nodded enthusiastically. 'Oh, yes!'

'Watch out that you don't grow fins,' said Sophie, 'with all the fish you gobble up.'

Swantje disappeared into the kitchen and Bruno said to the barman, 'We need to speak to the police.'

Lührsen put a beer glass into the dishwasher, saying, 'The police? Are you joking?' He didn't wait for the answer but burst out laughing.

'Our mothers are being held in Wohlfarth's factory,' said Sophie.

Swantje came out of the kitchen, her eyes popping.

'What mothers are being held?' she asked, putting a plate of fish and potato salad in front of Nicholas.

'One is, anyway,' said Sophie.

'Emily nearly drowned, and her mother too,' said Nicholas, spilling fishy gunge out of his mouth. 'Then the man with the boat came and took them out of the water.'

'Do you have to speak with your mouth full?' asked Sophie, shaking her head.

'Would you please inform the police?' Bruno asked the owner.

'I can't,' he said.

'Why not?' asked Sophie.

'Because there aren't any on the island,' said Hinnerk.

'So what happens if there's a crime?' asked Bruno.

'Ah, no,' said Swantje. 'That sort of thing don't happen here. We all knows each other here.'

'And in case of emergency, we have the coastguard,' said Hinnerk.

'Look, could you for goodness sake tell us what is going on?' said the owner.

Bruno had just opened his mouth when the door burst open and Wohlfarth came tumbling in.

'There you are!' he gasped. 'We searched the whole beach for you.'

'So you can lock us up too, right?' said Sophie, making a face. But her expression cleared when she saw who was coming in behind Wohlfarth. 'Emily!'

Emily looked serious but calm. She was wearing a pair of trousers that were far too long for her and a blue and white striped fisherman's shirt.

'What's the story with your mother?' asked Bruno.

'She's fine,' said Emily.

'We had a bit of an accident, unfortunately,' said Wohlfarth to the barman. 'Emily, the daughter of one of my … eh, one of my … students misjudged the tide and she was very nearly swept out to sea. Her mother tried to save her.'

'We were nearly drowned,' said Emily.

'These kids wanted me to call the police. They say someone is being held in the factory.'

'Nobody is being held against their will,' said Wohlfarth. 'Isn't that right, Emily?'

Emily nodded. 'That's right. It was all a mistake,' she said.

✳

That night, the children did not stay with Vibke Paulsen but in a stuffy little attic room in Dune View that had not been occupied for years and smelt unpleasantly of mothballs and musty bedclothes.

Nicholas was delighted to find a mousetrap under his bed with a mummified mouse in it.

'Can I keep it, Sofa?' he asked.

'No,' said Sophie as she tried to open the skylight to let in some fresh air.

'I could swap it for my jellyfish,' said Nicholas, taking a lump of gunk out of his pocket.

'Eeek!' yelped Sophie.

'I want to know about your mother,' said Bruno. He was disappointed that the whole rescue plan had come to nothing.

Emily shrugged. 'She says she has thought it all over, and she really doesn't want to come home just yet. The only reason she wanted to leave was that she wanted to see me, and now that she has, everything is fine again.'

'Do you believe that?' asked Sophie, spitting on a hanky to wipe Nicholas's dirty hands.

'Why would she lie?' asked Emily, lying down on one of the beds and pulling the cover up over her.

Bruno yawned. 'Another few nights and we'll have slept in every house on this island.'

'Well, I'm not interested in doing that, thank you very much,' said Sophie. 'I'm looking forward to my own bed.'

Hinnerk was not only to take the children to the mainland in the morning but to accompany them by train to Hamburg.

'So that nothing happens to you,' Wohlfarth had said with a smile. 'You children are our most precious commodities.'

'Maybe it's not as bad as we thought,' said Emily, thinking back on those words. 'They all seem to like it. Wohlfarth let me take a peek into the recreation room. The mothers were playing Old Maid or Canasta, and some of them were watching TV or reading. They have to go to bed at half past ten.'

'Yeah, but *your* mother wanted to leave,' insisted Bruno.

'Yes, but you can't take my mother seriously. She likes to make a big deal out of everything.'

'Oh, well. Goodnight everyone,' said Sophie.

'Goodnight Mousie,' said Nicholas softly to his mouse corpse.

Chapter 18

Swantje woke the children early the next morning. She had laid breakfast for them downstairs. Nicholas was very disappointed to find that there was no fried fish, only rolls and jam.

'Shall I pack you something for the journey?' asked Swantje.

'That'd be nice,' Bruno was saying when the door burst open and Emily's mother fell in.

'Thank God you're still here!'

She waved a carrier bag. 'I washed your skirt and blouse last night, Emily,' she said, and added with a smile, 'and I ironed them this morning.' She took a white blouse out of the bag. 'Only it's got a bit crumpled.'

Emily took the blouse from her mother and said with a beam, 'You've done a great job, thanks, Mum. I'll just go and put these things on.' She disappeared behind the counter.

'And you really don't want to come with us?' Bruno asked Emily's mother.

'It was very nice of you to try to help me,' said Emily's mother, shaking her head. 'But no, it's not necessary any more.'

Emily came waltzing out in her skirt and blouse and gave her mother the trousers and fisherman's shirt she had been wearing.

'You can take these. I think they belong to Sven-Ole.'

Susie rolled the things up and stuffed them into the carrier bag. Then she hugged her daughter and said, 'I have to go. Class is just starting. See you soon, darling, very soon!'

Emily felt something damp on her cheek. Surely her mother couldn't be crying? But before she could ask, her mother ran to the door and almost bumped right into Hinnerk, who was just coming in.

He tipped his cap at them and said, 'Mornin', mornin', are you all ready to set sail?'

Sophie gulped down the last of her orange juice and answered, 'Aye, aye, cap'n.'

'But what about Mama?' asked Nicholas, watching a fly that had got stuck on the jam pot.

'We'll see Mum later,' said Sophie. 'But now we're going on a boat. Won't that be lovely?'

'Well, maybe not exactly lovely,' said Hinnerk. 'The sea is right choppy today.'

'Choppy!' cried Bruno, alarmed. 'Not again!'

'Ah, just a bit of a swell, that's all,' said Hinnerk.

Bruno was sorry he'd eaten those two rolls with jam. He could have saved them for later.

It was only a few paces from Dune View to the pier. The seagulls were all lined up, as if they'd come to wave the children goodbye. For the first time, Bruno noticed a sleek motor boat that looked a bit out of place among all the smaller boats. It said *Margarethe* in gold letters along the hull.

'She's cool,' he said. 'Who does she belong to?'

'Wohlfarth,' said Hinnerk. 'His mother's name was Margarethe.'

'His mother was called Margarethe?' asked Emily. 'I thought she was dead.'

'He's had this yacht for ever,' said Hinnerk. 'And anyway, you can always call a boat after a dead person if you want to. In their memory.'

'Of course. I just find it a bit odd that ...'

'What?' asked Bruno.

'Oh, nothing, forget it.'

Bruno still couldn't see why there was anything strange about naming a boat after your mother, but he couldn't think about that now. He was feeling sick. He was feeling sicker than he had ever felt in his life. The fishing boat was going up and down with every wave, bobbing and swaying. It made a rollercoaster ride seem like a walk in the park.

Hinnerk was standing stoutly at the helm, working hard to keep his boat on course. Emily was clutching her skirt, which was being blown up all the time by the stiff wind. And Sophie sat with her eyes closed, crouched up against the wall of the boat. She didn't dare to move in case she threw up. Only Nicholas cheered happily every time water came sloshing over the deck.

After the most vile sixty minutes of their lives, the children came ashore in Südersiel, their legs still wobbling under them. They were very glad to get into a train that sat nice and quietly on its tracks and showed no signs of pitching from side to side.

The journey was uneventful. Emily looked out of the window, Nicholas slept and Sophie chewed her nails. Bruno was reading a boxing magazine that he'd had in his rucksack, while Hinnerk perused the catalogue of a Hamburg ship chandlers. He needed a new engine.

'These things are not exactly cheap,' he said, taking a map of Hamburg out of his bag.

'Could I take a peek, please?' asked Emily.

'You know your way home from Hamburg, don't you?' asked Hinnerk.

'Sure we do,' said Bruno. 'My train goes from platform twelve at a quarter past ten.'

'We're leaving from the same platform,' said Sophie, 'only twenty minutes later.'

'It's just that my aunt lives in Hamburg,' said Emily. 'I thought I might call in and see her. But I'm not sure I can remember exactly where her street is.'

Hinnerk passed her the map of Hamburg and, a few moments later, the train came into Hamburg Central Station.

The fisherman said goodbye to the children on the platform. 'Maybe we'll meet again some time,' he said. He had no idea how soon.

Sophie and Bruno were about to make their way to platform twelve, but Emily caught Sophie by the arm and said, 'I want you to come with me.'

'To see your aunt?' asked Bruno. 'What would we want to do that for?'

'I want to go home!' moaned Nicholas.

'Just for a few minutes,' said Emily. 'Please. I'm scared to go by myself.'

'Oh, for goodness' sake,' said Sophie impatiently. 'Where do you want us to go?'

But she followed Emily out of the station.

'Listen,' Emily said. 'After Kruschke rescued me and my mum, Wohlfarth wanted to speak to us. While we were waiting for him in his office, I saw this letter lying on his desk. It was addressed to a Margarethe Wohlfarth.'

'You think that's his mother?' asked Bruno. 'It could easily be some other relation of his.'

'Or it could be an old letter,' said Sophie. 'He reveres his mother. He has probably kept all kinds of things that belonged to her.'

'No,' said Emily. 'I could tell by the post code. They used to have four digits, right? The five-digit ones only came in a while back, so it can't be an old letter.'

'Did you see what street?' asked Bruno.

'Yes,' said Emily. 'The street was "Am Krahenberg".'

'And where's that, when it's at home?' asked Bruno.

'It's in an area of the city called Blankenese,' said Emily.

'Well, so what?' said Sophie. 'Even if we did find this Margarethe Wohlfarth, what do you want with her?'

Emily shrugged. 'I don't exactly know. But somehow, I don't really believe my mother when she says everything is fine. She was crying when she said goodbye to me.'

'Oh, that's nothing,' said Bruno. 'My mother roared her head off on my first day at school. Mothers are just like that.'

'But mine *isn't* like that,' said Emily. 'She's always in a mess and terrible things happen to her, but I have never seen her crying.'

'I want an ice cream!' squawked Nicholas.

'Later,' said Sophie.

'It won't take long,' said Emily, seeming very sure of herself. 'I really have this feeling that I have to go there. I feel that is the way to find out what on earth this whole mother school thing is about.'

'Hmm,' said Bruno. 'Well, I suppose, I have no plans. My father thinks I'm still on this school trip.'

'And George won't be home until Friday evening,' said Sophie.

'So, off we go to Blankenese!'

'What about my ice cream?' asked Nicholas.

'You'll get it when we arrive,' Emily promised him. 'They have the nicest ones there.'

When they arrived at Blankenese, Sophie said, 'What fabulous houses they have here!'

'It must be all rich people,' said Bruno.

Nicholas wasn't interested in fine houses belonging to rich people. He'd had enough of all this going around the place. He wanted his ice cream. Sophie bought him a big chocolate ice cream, which was not only especially delicious, but also especially expensive, but at least it shut her little brother up for a while.

They walked along a street of very fancy villas with wrought-iron railings and rhododendron hedges. Emily stopped at a garden gate. 'This must be it. Number 66.'

Number 66 was a brilliant white villa with two black marble pillars in front. Beside the brass doorbell on the gate, instead of a name-card, there were just two intertwined Ws.

'We've come to the right place,' said Sophie. 'I recognise that logo. I saw it on the neck of my Aunt Anna.'

All the same, Emily felt a bit wobbly as she pressed on the doorbell. 'What'll we say?' she asked as the gate hummed open.

'We'll think of something when we meet the lady,' said Bruno.

It wasn't a lady that they saw now, however, but a gentleman, standing in the open gateway and giving them a suspicious look. He was wearing a dark jacket over a striped waistcoat.

'Do you think he's a butler?' Emily whispered to Sophie. 'I've only seen those on the television.'

They were walking along a paved path, guarded on either side by trim box trees, towards the house.

'What do you want?' asked the man, not sounding too friendly.

Nicholas hid behind Sophie. She spoke up bravely: 'We'd like to speak to Frau Margarethe Wohlfarth, please.'

'In connection with what?' said the man.

'We have a message for her from Walther Wohlfarth.'

'From her son?' asked the man with a frown.

'Exactly,' said Emily, giving Bruno a triumphant look.

'Just a moment, please.'

The butler disappeared.

'Didn't I tell you it's the mother!'

The butler reappeared.

'Madam wishes you to …'

He made a movement with his hand that managed to seem snide rather than inviting, but nevertheless beckoned them on. They crossed a hallway tiled in black and white and entered a room with a large bay window.

A red satin armchair stood in front of the window, and in the armchair, a black-clad person sat bolt upright. On her protruding bosom there gleamed a large gold medallion. Her knobbly hand rested on the silver handle of a walking stick. At her feet lay some kind of grey-brown mop or duster.

'It's her,' murmured Emily. 'It's the woman in the portrait.'

It was certainly true that the woman sitting here bore some resemblance to the portrait that hung in Wohlfarth's study. Except that her features, which looked soft and gentle in the picture, were stony. Either the painter had flattered her or age had made a monster of the woman. That's exactly what she looked like: a monster out of a nightmare, eyes as hard and penetrating as marbles, a chin that fell in a cascade of bulges and squeezed itself into a stiff collar, a mouth that looked as if it had been drawn with a ruler and a nose as hooked and as pointy as a parrot's.

The ruler-straight mouth opened and a voice as sharp as a razor, so sharp that you could positively see it cutting the air, said, 'What have you got to tell me?'

Before any of the children got a chance to answer, her marble eyes fell on Nicholas. He was standing there with his ice cream in his hand, his mouth open in horror.

'Alfred, take that ice cream from the child before there's a catastrophe.'

Before Nicholas knew what was happening, the butler had snatched the ice cream out of his hand. He held it out in front of him like something that stank and left the room with it.

'My ice cream! I want my ice cream!'

At that moment, the mop came to life. It yapped at Nicholas and snapped at his leg with piranha-like teeth

'Sit, Henry!' called Frau Wohlfarth, and the tangled thing rolled itself up again and lay at her feet.

'What was that?' asked Sophie in disgust.

'That is Henry the Fourth,' said Frau Wohlfarth.

She poked at the mop with her stick and a head with a flattened nose and bulging eyes appeared, with a bow in its topnotch.

'A Pekinese. Also known as a palace dog. In the past, only the Emperors of China were allowed to own this breed.'

'Just as well,' muttered Bruno.

'Well, boy,' said Frau Wohlfarth, turning towards Nicholas.

'What was that you said?'

He had stepped back, terrified at having been attacked by the dog, but he spoke up bravely now and said, 'I want my ice cream back.'

'Well, maybe you would *like* it back,' said Frau Wahlfarth. 'But the word "want" does not belong in the vocabulary of a child.'

She gave him a look of pure disgust and added, 'And what's more, your nose is running.'

Nicholas took a slimy mess out of his pocket.

'That's a jellyfish for my collection,' he announced proudly and stuffed the thing back into his pocket.

'And this,' he said, pulling something out of the other pocket, 'this is Mousie.' He stroked the mummified mouse tenderly.

'Alfred! Quick!' shouted the old woman, rapping impatiently on the floor with her stick. 'Bring a dustpan and brush.'

Alfred hurried in with what had been ordered.

'Empty your pockets at once!' said Frau Wohlfarth to Nicholas.

He started to roar. 'But I want to keep Mousie!'

'Did you use the word "want"?' The old woman had stood up and was towering threateningly over Nicholas. 'I do not want to hear that word again, or I will wash your mouth out with soap.'

This was supposed to be a wonderful mother – the best in the world?

Emily gazed incredulously at the old woman who was giving Nicholas such an evil look that he quickly threw his jellyfish and his mouse onto the dustpan.

Wrinkling his nose, Alfred disappeared with it.

'Well, good riddance!' grunted the old woman happily. Then she turned to Bruno and Sophie and said, 'So, then, tell me why you are here, and get a move on about it. I haven't got all day.'

'Your son asked us to say hello from him. We met him yesterday.'

'In America?'

'What's America got to do with it?' asked Bruno, puzzled. 'He's here in Germany.'

Frau Wohlfarth pointed her walking stick at Bruno.

'Nonsense! My son lives in New York. He works for the Walker, Winehouse and Winston Bank, which will shortly be the Walker, Winehouse and Welfare Bank. And do you know why? Because old Winston has died, and my boy is to be a shareholder. This year.' A short, almost imperceptible smile hovered over her awful face. 'And if you are any good at English, you will know that Welfare is the word in English for our honourable surname.'

'Well, then, it must be a different Walther Wohlfarth,' said Sophie. 'So sorry to have disturbed you.' She was holding Nicholas close, and he was crying softly.

'There is only one,' said the old woman, 'and that is my son.'

She moved over to a sideboard on which there stood several silver-framed photographs. She took one of them in her hand then stepped towards the children. Now that she was so close to them, they got an unpleasant smell from her. A mixture of cologne, old floor cloths and dust. She held the photo out to them.

'This is my son, Walther Wohlfarth Junior.'

It was a photo of the Wohlfarth they knew. He was wearing a dark three-piece suit and was sitting at a large desk. Behind him could be seen in large gold letters the words 'Walker, Wine…'

'That's the fellow we mean all right,' said Bruno, 'and I recognise that desk too. But it's not in New York. It's on Nordfall. That's a little island in the North Sea.'

The old woman waved her stick brusquely. 'I know where that island is. That's where my husband's munitions factory was. After he died, my son took it into his head to make toys there. Even though I had spent a fortune on his education. Have you any idea what a boarding school in England costs?'

The children shook their heads.

'Of course not. You don't look as if your parents could afford something like that.' She gave a derisive laugh. 'I told him that was nonsense. Who needs toys? The children today are all spoilt anyway, aren't they?'

She bent down to Nicholas and chucked him on the chin.

The butler came in. 'Would you like some refreshment, madam?'

'That's a good idea, Alfred. Please bring me a glass of bitters and a hot chocolate for Henry. And for the children, water with a shot of cider vinegar. It's refreshing and slimming.' She gave Sophie a cutting look.

Alfred bowed and left the room, and Frau Wohlfarth sat back into her armchair.

'And I was, of course, right, as always,' she continued. 'He went bust with that silly kiddy stuff. But then came this invitation from New York. And there he climbed the ladder very quickly from lowly employee to shareholder.'

'Your son is not producing toys any more,' said Bruno. 'That's correct. But he *is* still on the island. He has a school there.'

'A school for terrible mothers,' Emily added.

'Nonsense!' said Frau Wohlfarth, taking an envelope out of her pocket. 'I get a letter from him on the first of the month, every month, like clockwork.'

Emily looked at Bruno.

'Could I have a look at that?' asked Bruno, and the old lady handed him the envelope.

'It is postmarked New York all right, but that means nothing.'

'What do you mean, boy?'

'I just mean that he could easily have written the letter on Nordfall and then had it sent to someone in New York, who could put a stamp on it and stick it in the post.'

'So that you would think he was a banker on Wall Street,' said Sophie.

And Emily added, 'But in fact, he is on Nordfall, where he teaches mothers how to make custard and build sandcastles.'

Alfred came in with a tray on which stood four water glasses, a steaming bowl and a shot glass.

Nicholas shook his head violently when Alfred held out the vinegar water to him and gave Henry the Fourth an envious glance as he slurped his chocolate.

'Trust us,' said Bruno. 'We've seen it with our own eyes.'

The old woman knocked back her bitter shot in one gulp and gave Alfred the empty glass. Then she stood up.

'If you are right, and these monstrous suggestions of yours are indeed the truth, then I will personally tan Walther Wohlfarth Junior's bottom for him.'

Chapter 19

Susie was sitting at her desk, puzzling over the question, *How do I react if my child lies?*

> A: I impose a one-week TV ban
> B: I try to find out why the child has lied
> C: I lie to the child myself, so that he or she experiences how it feels to be lied to
> D: I wash his mouth out with soap

Emily didn't tell lies. Or did she? Could you call it a lie when she pumped her mother up with optimism before she had a job interview, saying, 'You're good, Mum, you just need to believe in yourself.'

'I'm not one bit good,' murmured Susie. 'Otherwise I wouldn't be here.'

Earth Mother, who was sitting next to her, hissed, 'Quiet! I'm trying to concentrate.'

Some of the mothers were bent over their worksheets. Others were scratching their heads. Sophie's mother was smiling in that self-satisfied way she had. She was sure she'd tick all the right answers.

Susie ticked B and looked at the next question. *My child gets a bad mark at school. How do I react?*

> A: I say, 'That's what happens when you don't study'
> B: I blame the teacher because he hasn't managed to teach my child properly
> C: I promise I'll practise with my child before the next test
> D: I thrash his behind for him

Thrashing a child's behind? Who would do a thing like that? Susie couldn't remember ever having smacked Emily. She did remember once giving her a tap on the bottom when she ran out into the middle of the road and nearly got run over. But that was years ago.

'These questions are totally daft,' muttered Susie, and Bruno's mother whispered, 'You can say that again.'

'Quiet!' called Ramona Bottle. 'Anyone caught talking will have to hand in their paper immediately.'

She stood behind a lectern and every now and then she looked over her glasses at them, checking that nobody was copying. In between times, she filed her nails, getting ready to paint them with a pearly nail varnish.

That won't do you the slightest bit of good, thought Susie, rather meanly. They'd all noticed immediately that their practical theory teacher was in love with the director. But Wohlfarth took absolutely no notice of polished nails or of lovesick eyelid-batting either.

The last question on the worksheet was, What do you think makes a good mother? You were supposed to write at least two pages. Susie didn't think for long before writing:

A good mother puts the life of her child before her own. She is ready to make any sacrifice if it does her child good.

She crossed out 'any' and wrote 'many' in its place. A mother who sacrificed everything wouldn't be any good either. Only a happy mother could be a good mother.

Susie was a happy mother, wasn't she? After all, she had saved Emily's life. Kruschke had used that to blackmail her. When Susie thought about it, icy chills ran up her spine. First he had pulled her out of the water. Then he had pointed at Emily, who was struggling and being carried further and further from shore. 'I can save her, but only if you shut your mouth and don't make any more stupid moves,' he'd said.

In this situation, Susie would have promised to take the moon down from the sky. 'I'll do anything you want, but please, please, take my child out of that sea!'

And now Emily was on her way back to Berlin. She'd probably move in with her father until Susie was back home. And she would probably discover that this girlfriend of his wasn't so stupid after all, but was actually quite nice. And not as disorganised as her own mother.

Susie sighed.

'Time's up, please hand up your papers,' called Ramona Bottle, tapping a pen against the lectern. 'But quietly, if you please.'

'What did you put for number 6?' asked Bruno's mother.

'B, but I'm not sure that's right,' Susie whispered back.

Ramona Bottle gathered in all the papers. 'You can take your break now,' she said. 'Afterwards we'll have the results, and we can discuss your answers.'

'Do we have to?' asked Earth Mother. 'Is it not enough if you just tell us what the right answers are?'

'Exactly,' agreed Sophie's mother. 'All this eternal picking stuff over. Why not just give us our grades and be done with it?'

'You'll get an A, anyway,' said Bruno's mother jealously. 'No skin off your nose.'

'I agree, it's just a waste of time,' Fitness Mother chimed in. She was doing a few knee-bends as she spoke. 'We could be jogging on the beach instead.'

'Or doing our homework,' said Clingy Mum.

Bruno's mother pushed her way to the front. 'Sven-Ole recorded a boxing match last night. I have to watch it before I go to training.'

She had not only learnt lots of boxing rules off by heart, but lately she'd actually been hitting a punchbag, 'to get a feel for it,' she said.

The mothers all started complaining now. 'I've had it up to here with this practical theory stuff,' Clingy Mum moaned.

Ramona Bottle retreated behind her lectern and reached for her bell.

'Quiet!' she cried. 'Silence at once, or everyone will stay back after class.'

Earth Mother twirled her finger at her temple, to show that she thought Ramona Bottle was a nutcase, and said, 'Oh, wow! Really?'

'I'll report you all!' cried Ramona Bottle, getting red in the face and swinging her bell like crazy.

'Oh, let her be,' said Susie to Clingy Mum. 'Come on, let's go to the beach.'

At that moment, the door opened and in came Wohlfarth.

'What's going on here?' he asked.

Ramona Bottle was close to tears by this stage.

'They won't do their work!' she said with a snuffle.

'That's not true,' argued Bruno's mother. 'We've just spent two hours filling in those damned tests, but there is only so much we can take.'

She grabbed one of the pages and read it out. 'You want to take your child to the toilet, but the child says he doesn't need to go. Then he wets himself. What's the right thing to do?'

She looked at Wohlfarth. 'Thank God I have that phase behind me anyway.' She scrunched up the paper and threw it towards the wastepaper basket.

'Exactly! Bottle's classes have nothing to do with real life,' cried Sophie's mother, scrunching up the next sheet.

'It's as dry as a soya burger,' Earth Mother added.

Wohlfarth raised his hands in a conciliatory gesture. 'Calm down, please.'

One last ball of paper flew through the air.

'I understand. You want a lesson that has a more direct bearing on your needs. Is that right?'

They all nodded.

'All right, then. I'll call a teachers' meeting. You can have two hours to work quietly, and at lunchtime I'll let you know what we have decided.'

He made a gesture to Ramona Bottle and the two of them left the room.

Not surprisingly, the quiet time he had prescribed was anything but quiet.

'We have to think of something,' said Wohlfarth later in his office. 'Only contented students learn things.'

'Well, I've had no complaints,' said Sven-Ole in a self-satisfied tone.

'Me neither,' said Vibke Paulsen.

Ramona Bottle sat there like a bundle of misery.

'What is it, Kruschke?'

Kruschke was opening his book of grades. 'They've all got a D or an E from me,' he said.

'That's impossible,' said Wohlfarth. 'You're doing something wrong!'

'I'm not getting it wrong. The mothers are doing it all wrong,' said Kruschke. 'In model construction, they've all scored F! Not one of them can distinguish between magnetic steering, infrared steering and programmed steering. Not to mention what they can't tell you about a dynamic drive in relation to a rear-action drive. Which is the easiest thing in the world.'

'So you say,' said Vibke Paulsen, 'but it's all Greek to me.'

Wohlfarth pulled his fingers through his hair in irritation. 'Look, we're not going to get anywhere with this.'

'I've been saying that from the start, boss,' said Kruschke. 'If you'd listened to me, we'd never have got involved in all this nonsense in the first place.'

'Right, and have you got any better suggestions?' asked Vibke Paulsen.

'As far as I'm concerned, the whole business with these mothers is already up the spout. Look, can't you see how fantastic my Annas are by comparison with all this? Earth Mother's husband wants to divorce her, he is so taken with his Anna. He's not getting any of those wholegrain nut roasts. We don't need the mothers at all.'

'So what do you suggest we do with them?' asked Sven-Ole. 'Should we wring their necks, or what?'

Kruschke's left eyelid was hopping, but he said nothing.

Wohlfarth cleared his throat. 'I have a suggestion.'

❁

The atmosphere was tense in the dining room that lunchtime. And not because there was fish yet again. No. Rumours were flying. Some people claimed that Ramona Bottle had fled. Others said that Vibke Paulsen had had such a row with Wohlfarth that she had given her notice. Still others claimed that Wohlfarth's institute for mother improvement was going to close that very day.

Quite a few of the mothers thought this was a shame.

'I've been looking forward to getting my certificate,' said Sophie's mother. 'I know I'll get an A in sandcastle building.'

Kruschke came down the steps from Wohlfarth's office.

'I have something to tell you,' he said. 'The staff has decided that there will be no lessons this afternoon. Instead, the director would like to invite you on a picnic. We're going to have a nice stroll on the beach, and then we will meet at a certain place that I can't disclose to you just yet.'

The mothers were not exactly thrilled at this news.

'I hate picnics,' said Bruno's mother to Susie. 'There's always some creature that stings you, and there's sand in your grub.'

'Exactly,' said Clingy Mum. 'It's always terribly uncomfortable.'

'Still, it's better than building model aeroplanes with Kruschke,' said Earth Mother. 'I stuck my wings on the wrong way round last time and he nearly had a heart attack.'

'Well, at least he can't do much to us on a picnic,' said Bruno's mother.

She was wrong. Very wrong.

❀

While the mothers, not in the best of humour, were setting off on their picnic, the children were on board a boat yet again. This time it was the *Henry I*, a yacht belonging to Frau Wohlfarth. They had boarded at Brunsbüttel, where Alfred the butler had changed his clothes for the second time. When they had left Blankenese to travel along by the Elbe in Frau Wohlfarth's elderly Mercedes, he had swapped his butler's outfit for a chauffeur's uniform. And now he appeared on the yacht looking quite the sailor in a captain's jacket and peaked cap.

Standing in the bow was Frau Wohlfarth, looking like the Angel of Death. Her skirt was blowing in the wind. She was hanging onto her stick with one hand; with the other, she held an old-fashioned telescope to her eye and was shouting directions.

'Twenty degrees to starboard! Ten degrees to port. A surge in the mainsail.'

Henry the Fourth was wearing a little yellow oilcloth coat with a matching bow in his topnotch. He slithered from one side of the deck to the other with every heave of the boat.

Suddenly old Wohlfarth sliced the air with her walking stick, waving it like a rapier. 'There it is! Nordfall!'

The children weren't particularly interested. It was their third time to see the island.

Alfred moored the boat, leapt ashore and reached out to offer his arm to help the old woman to disembark.

'This won't take long,' she said to him. 'You can have

something over in the guesthouse, but nothing alcoholic, if you please.'

Then she used her crook to gesture to the children to come with her. Bruno was still a bit light-headed from the voyage, and Nicholas was whingeing because he was hungry.

'Come on. There's no time for dawdling about.'

※

'Oh, lord,' muttered Sophie's mother. 'How long do we have to go traipsing around here? I'm thirsty.'

It was hot that day, very hot. Now and again a fresh breeze blew in from the sea, but the sun beat mercilessly down on the mothers and the white sand dazzled them.

Kruschke led the way, constantly wiping the sweat off his forehead.

'Not much longer,' he called over his shoulder. 'We're nearly there.'

'He's been saying that for the past hour.' Bruno's mother was fizzing with irritation.

'I'm looking forward to a nice piece of cake,' said Clingy Mum, who was small and fat.

'And a nice cup of coffee,' added Earth Mother, who was tall and thin.

For once, the two of them were in agreement.

Susie took up the rear. She was the only one who wasn't complaining. She had taken her sandals off and was enjoying the feeling of the sand between her toes and wading through the little water channels. The water was quite warm, and transparent shrimps and tiny fishes swam in it.

She shaded her eyes with her hand and looked out to sea. A freighter was sailing by on the horizon. Seagulls were screeching overhead.

Why can't I just enjoy it all? thought Susie to herself. She felt in her pocket for Porky. There he was! Even though she wasn't superstitious, she somehow felt a lot safer with him there. She laughed softly at herself. What on earth could happen on a picnic?

A grey-green mound came into view. As they came closer to it, the mothers realised it was a bunker, half smothered on the landward side by a high dune and half sunk into the sand on the seaward.

'It looks kind of spooky,' said Sophie's mother.

'Maybe there are bodies in it,' said Suspicious Mum, and her pointy nose got pointier.

Kruschke gave a dismissive wave. 'Bodies! Don't be ridiculous. The most you'll come across in there would be courting couples. It's nice and dark and cosy.'

'Cosy?' said Bruno's mother, turning away. 'I could think of a more comfortable spot.'

Kruschke frowned, as if he was trying to decide whether he should reveal a secret. 'Apparently, some high-ranking navy officer is supposed to have hidden a fortune here, in the last days of the war. Old jewellery, silver cutlery, valuable paintings …'

Now the mothers looked a lot more interested.

'He was trying to safeguard it from the enemy troops, but it didn't do him any good, because before he could get it out again, he went down with all hands. just here off Nordfall.'

'But surely they came looking for it?' asked Suspicious Mum, whose eyes had lit up greedily when she heard the word 'silver'.

Kruschke shook his head. 'Nobody knows except me. And I only found out a few days ago. Completely by chance.'

'How do you get in?' asked Clingy Mum, rattling the wooden door.

'It's just a bit stiff,' said Kruschke.

Clingy Mum threw her whole weight against the door, and it opened with a squeak of protest.

❋

After they had left Alfred at Dune View with a cup of tea, old Frau Wohlfarth marched determinedly through the village towards the factory. The Pekinese wasn't doing too well on his stubby little legs, so she had pressed her darling into Sophie's arms. Sophie wrinkled her nose. Henry the Fourth smelt of wet dog. Aristocratic or not, wet dogs do not smell nice.

When they reached the mesh fence, they found that the gate was locked with a rusty chain and padlock. This didn't bother the old woman. Her anger lent her superhuman powers. She raised her stick and hit the lock. The padlock fell apart and the gate swung open.

'Did you see that?' Bruno whispered to Sophie. 'Karate with a walking stick!'

Shaking with anger, Frau Wohlfarth marched up the drive to the factory. But she couldn't open the door to the workshop with her stick. Whether she liked it or not, she was going to have to ring the bell. The shrill sound echoed hollowly inside the building. For a long time nothing happened. Then the door opened a crack and Vibke Paulsen stuck her head out.

'What can I do for you?' she asked, looking at Frau Wohlfarth. Only then did she notice the children, and her eyes opened wide.

'What are you lot doing here again?'

'I would like to speak to my son. Immediately.'

Vibke Paulsen's mouth hung open.

'But you're …' she stammered.

'Dead? As you see, I am quite alive. Now, please, get out of my way!'

Vibke Paulsen stood stock-still in shock, so the old woman simply pushed her aside with her stick and walked on in.

'But you can't just come marching in here,' Vibke Paulsen shouted after her.

'I most certainly can!' announced Frau Wohlfarth, striding through the factory floor like a kanga-hammer. Now and again she sliced a doll's head off with her stick or ripped open a stuffed animal with the pointy end of it.

'Kiddy rubbish!' she roared. 'Silly nonsense. Complete waste of time.'

As she went past the conveyor belts that had been turned into tables, she asked sharply, 'What's going on here? Coffee mornings?'

She stopped when she got to the staircase leading up to Wohlfarth's office and turned to the children.

'Is he up there?' she asked.

Emily nodded.

'In his father's office! Unbelievable!'

Just as Frau Wohlfarth was about to climb the stairs, Vibke Paulsen stopped her. She was holding a doll's head in her hand, one that had been chopped off. The head had red cheeks and blond plaits with a pink ribbon.

'Look!' she said. 'This is Grete. She was our most successful model. She wore a genuine traditional costume, a dirndl.'

'You don't mean to tell me,' said Frau Wohlfarth turning around, 'that my son named a DOLL ...' She practically spat the word. 'That he named a *doll* after me? Absolutely incredible!'

'Exactly,' said Vibke Paulsen. 'I cannot believe that anyone would call anything after you!' She added under her breath, 'Except maybe a rhinoceros.'

By now the old woman had arrived at Wohlfarth's door. She didn't bother to knock. She just swung the door open. Wohlfarth was sitting at his desk, directly under the portrait of his mother. Ramona Bottle was standing beside him, handing him a folder. Sven-Ole was lounging in a chair, reading a manual on child-rearing.

'I have a question,' he was saying. 'Parents who have had it up to here with their daughters, could they ever feel *sunny* about things, do you think? D'you get it, d'you get it – SON-ny!'

When he caught sight of Frau Wohlfarth, the laughter stuck in his throat.

It's just like when you're watching a DVD, thought Emily, and you press the Stop button. Everyone had frozen to the spot. All eyes were on the apparition in the doorway.

The first to move was Sven-Ole. He looked from the old woman to the picture over Wohlfarth's desk and then back to her.

Wohlfarth had gone white as a sheet. 'Mother ... you ... what are you doing here?'

Frau Wohlfarth took a step towards her son and rested both hands on the desk. Her parrot-nosed face shot forward. 'You're on the board of the biggest bank in New York, isn't that right? You are engaged to the owner's daughter, right? You spend your free time in an exclusive golf club. Right?'

With every 'right' Wohlfarth collapsed. Three times altogether. Ramona Bottle collapsed just the once, and that was when she heard the word 'engaged'.

'Did I teach you how to lie like that? Did I teach you to go behind your own mother's back? Speak to me!'

'I didn't want to disappoint you, mother,' said Wohlfarth. His voice shook. 'I knew you wouldn't stand for all this.' He stretched his arms out to indicate what she would not stand for. 'You never had any time for toys.'

'For a very good reason,' Frau Wohlfarth spat. 'Children should not play. They should study. So that they do not grow up to be losers. Like you.'

'I never owned as much as a teddy,' said Wohlfarth softly.

'Yes, you did. Your aunt sent you one. But I threw it away,' said the old woman.

Wohlfarth leapt to his feet. 'Now I remember. He had these funny button eyes and he was so soft. I used to take him to bed with me, but you took him away from me. You are *appalling*. You are the world's worst mother.'

Frau Wohlfarth reached out and whacked her son a resounding clip on the ear. He sat back on his chair and started to wail. Ramona Bottle stood beside him and stroked his shoulders helplessly, as the old woman released a barrage of shouts and screams at him. The most harmless insults she hurled at him were 'loser', 'fathead' and 'dishrag'.

Sven-Ole gestured to the others and they left the office.

Vibke Paulsen, who had been listening all the while on the other side of the door asked, horrified, 'Am I dreaming, or is all this actually happening?'

'Seems to be actually happening,' said Sven-Ole. 'That's

supposed to have been the best mother in the world? She's a monster!'

'Where are our mothers?' asked Emily, when they were back on the factory floor.

Vibke Paulsen looked at her watch. 'Kruschke was to take over the afternoon classes today. He was going to take them to the beach to make kites and then fly them. Wohlfarth thought that'd be easier than the eternal model-aeroplane construction he goes on with. But they should be well back by now.'

'I feel a bit like Tom Sawyer in the cave,' said Susie, holding a candle up to the wall of the bunker to read the names that someone had scratched there.

Swantje and Hinnerk, it said, with a heart around the names.

'Nonsense,' said Sophie's mother. 'There aren't any passageways here where you could get lost.'

'And no stala-whatsits hanging from the ceiling,' said Bruno's mother.

'Stalagmites,' said Sophie's mother grandly.

'Stalactites,' Earth Mother corrected her. 'Stalagmites grow up from the floor.'

They were all holding candles that they had found, handily enough, at the entrance, and they were running around to see what they could find in the interior of the bunker.

'Well, have you found the treasure yet?' Earth Mother asked Clingy Mum, who was using a candle to light up the floor.

'There's a funny crack here,' she said by way of an answer.

'Don't be silly. There are all sorts of cracks and crevices everywhere here,' said Suspicious Mum, who was just lifting a battered old mattress up with her fingertips, but she found nothing more interesting than a few woodlice. The search for this supposed treasure was proving fruitless.

'I'm hungry,' said Bruno's mother. 'Didn't Kruschke say that Wohlfarth and the others were coming after us with the food? Maybe they're here by now.'

'I'd say Vibke Paulsen has baked apple pies,' said Clingy Mum. 'I love her apple pies.'

'What about the silver cutlery?' asked Suspicious Mum.

'Oh, I don't mind eating cake with my fingers,' said Susie with a laugh.

'OK, let's get out of here,' called Sophie's mother.

The big wooden door was only half-open, but then, out of nowhere, a dark figure pushed against it and, with a loud crashing sound, the bunker grew suddenly dark, apart from the light of the candles.

'The door is shut,' said Susie in surprise.

Sophie's mother ran up to it and rattled at it. 'It's locked!'

'Rubbish,' said Bruno's mother. 'It's just stuck. Let me at it. I've been training, and I'm strong.'

But all she got for her trouble was a sore arm.

'Kruschke!' she called. 'Kruschke, open up. This isn't funny!'

Nothing happened.

The others came closer and pushed against the door. They knocked. They shouted. All in vain.

'Maybe it's part of the lesson,' said Earth Mother. 'We're supposed to learn how to behave in a situation like this.'

'And how would you recommend we behave?' asked Clingy

Mum angrily. She'd been looking forward to a piece of cake and was not interested in playing games.

'We mustn't lose our nerve,' said Sophie's mother. 'If we keep quite quiet, nothing can happen to us.'

'We won't die of thirst anyway,' said Bruno's mother. 'There's plenty of water.' She pointed at a wall dripping with water.

'My feet are wet,' said Susie.

Then the others noticed it too. The floor of the bunker was damp. In some places, puddles were forming and getting slowly bigger.

'Does that mean this thing is going to fill up with water?' asked Bruno's mother, horrified.

'Surely not,' said Earth Mother. 'They couldn't have built the bunker in such a way that it would be underwater when the tide comes in. Our feet will get wet; that's all.'

Chapter 20

Bruno, Emily and Sophie were running along the beach. They had left Nicholas with Vibke Paulsen. She was reheating some fried fish from lunchtime for him.

Emily wasn't hungry. She was too unsettled. Something was wrong. She could sense it. Where on earth were the mothers?

Their footprints were still visible in places in the sand, but they were being slowly washed away by the tide. There was no sign of the women themselves anywhere.

'You'd think we'd at least see a few kites in the sky,' said Bruno.

'Maybe they were just too stupid to be able to make any,' said Sophie.

'Come on, let's climb up on the high dunes over there,' suggested Emily. 'We should be able to see something from there.'

They scrambled up a dune, but from there all they could see were more dunes. Sophie fell back onto the soft, warm sand and held her face up to the sun. It was supposed to be good for pimply skin. She closed her eyes, murmuring, 'They'll turn up. That many women can't just go missing.'

Emily sat down beside her, shaking the sand out of her skirt.

'But Frau Paulsen did say they should have been back long ago. Maybe they've gone exploring the mudflats and they've been caught by the tide.'

Bruno yawned. 'Kruschke was with them. He must be well up on the tides.'

❊

Kruschke did indeed know all about the tides. After he locked the door of the bunker, he checked his watch. Within an hour, the bunker would be full of water. Over the past fifty years, the sea had nibbled away at the north end of the island. This brought the bunker, which had originally been built in the middle of the dunes, closer and closer to the sea. What that meant, exactly, the ladies in the bunker would soon experience for themselves. By the time Wohlfarth noticed, at supper, that his pupils had disappeared, it would be too late.

He didn't feel the least bit guilty. Had he told the mothers to go scrabbling around in that bunker? It was their own greed, that typical female greed for money and glitter, that had lured them in and would be the ruination of them.

Back at the factory, he would say the mothers had sent him away so that they could have a bit of fun without any of the teaching staff around. Nobody would be able to enter the bunker again until after midnight when the tide would have gone out. He would be the first at the door and could unlock it secretly. Everyone on Nordfall knew that it got stuck easily, but nobody knew that he had the key to it.

Regrettably, none of the foolhardy ladies would live to tell the tale. It was a pity about none of them. There wasn't one among them who had ever taken him seriously.

There was only one person who respected and admired him. Only one. And he was on his way to her now. He wanted to tell her that victory was at hand, almost within their grasp. He didn't come back along the beach. Instead, he took the shortcut through the dunes.

❀

Bruno had climbed the next dune along and was taking a good look around. He needed to have a pee, and he didn't want the girls to see him. He'd just found a suitable spot when someone came hurrying along past him. It was Kruschke! Wasn't he supposed to be with the mothers? He was just about to call out, 'Hey, there,' but something made him hesitate, and instead he ran back to the girls.

'I've just seen Kruschke!' he said to them. 'But he is alone.'

'We'd better follow him, then,' said Emily. 'He must know where our mothers are.' Her heart had started to pound like mad.

Sophie sat up and pushed the hair out of her eyes. 'I don't know what good that'll do,' she said. 'I really couldn't be bothered.'

'Don't you want to see your mother?' asked Emily in surprise.

'Yes, but a few hours won't make any difference.'

But Emily had the feeling that it could make all the difference in the world.

❀

In the bunker, the water had reached thirty centimetres and was still climbing. The mothers had retreated to the back of the building where the floor was a good bit higher than it was near the door. They were all bunched up together.

'Hey, stop pushing.'

'I need a bit of space!'

'If you push, you're out.'

'Ho-ho, very funny.'

They had stuck the candles onto little ledges on the walls. There were no draughts, so they burnt steadily but alarmingly fast.

'I want out of here!' moaned Clingy Mum. 'I want to go home to my little Timmy. He misses me terribly, I'm sure of it.'

'Don't you believe it,' said Earth Mother bitterly. 'Our children seem to be managing very well without us. Otherwise, they'd have come looking for us.'

'They did,' said Susie quietly.

The others all turned to look at her. Her face looked eerily pale in the candlelight. 'My Emily was here,' she said.

'You're dreaming,' said Sophie's mother dismissively.

'Along with Bruno and Sophie and Nicholas.'

'What?' cried Bruno's mother. 'When? Where?'

'Sophie and Nicholas? Here? I don't believe it,' said Sophie's mother, shaking her head.

'I didn't get the whole story. We didn't have enough time. But they found out, through the … Annas, where we were.'

'Annas? You mean the childminders who have been looking after our children while we're here?' asked Earth Mother.

'Childminders. Yeah, right!' said Susie with a laugh. 'Do you know what they are? They're robots. Those dolls you've seen, they're all over the factory. They can talk, laugh, cry, belch. Kruschke had them made on a larger scale and he let them loose on our children.'

The mothers were all jabbering at the same time and they

never even noticed that the water had reached their little slope and was already lapping at their feet.

'Bruno, Emily and Sophie all found out independently of each other. And they also worked out that the dolls came from Wohlfarth's factory. So they came here.'

'And then what?' asked Sophie's mother.

'Wohlfarth told them what a great time everyone is having here and he sent them off again. But then they got suspicious so they came back.'

'And they had Nicholas with them the whole time?' asked Sophie's mother, horrified. 'He needs his afternoon nap.'

'Well, he didn't look too sleepy to me,' said Susie. 'Nice boy.'

'Yes, isn't he?' Sophie's mother smiled proudly.

'And your Sophie is one smart girl.'

'Do you think so? That's news to me.'

'Look, can't you tell us what happened?' insisted Bruno's mother. 'How is Bruno?'

'He's fine, except that he gets seasick. I wanted to go back to the mainland with the children, but the gate in the fence was locked. So then we tried to go by the beach, where the fence goes into the sea. And just as we had nearly managed to get around the fence by wading through the water, Emily was suddenly swept off her feet. When I tried to help her, I got carried away by the tide as well. If Kruschke hadn't turned up …' She stopped.

'So those stomach cramps of yours weren't real?' asked Earth Mother.

'No. I had to get away. I've wanted to get away the whole time.'

'We weren't exactly nice to you,' said Clingy Mum.

'It doesn't matter,' said Susie. 'The really annoying thing is that there's nobody to point a finger at that swine.'

'What swine?' asked someone.

'Kruschke, of course.'

'But I thought you said he rescued you,' said Clingy Mum. 'How does that make him a swine?'

'You'll find out soon enough,' said Susie. 'If you ask me, he is planning to drown us in here, like kittens.' And then Snivelling Susie started to panic. She laughed dementedly, her laughter echoing off the concrete walls and running, ice cold, down the spines of the other mothers.

❄

Kruschke was making his way unhurriedly towards the factory. The children had no bother catching up with him.

'Hello there!' called Bruno as Kruschke was just about to disappear through a side door. 'Wait a moment.'

Kruschke turned around. His face was bright red. It could be the heat. *Or anger*, thought Emily.

'Huh! You lot again!' said Kruschke. 'Aren't you supposed to be gone home long ago?'

Instead of answering, Sophie said, 'Where are our mothers?'

'Somewhere on the beach. They didn't feel like making kites and they sent me away. But they'll be back soon, I'm sure. It's nearly supper time.'

He went into a little room. It was clear this was his workshop. A smiling head lay on a table. It looked as if it had been scalped. Multicoloured wires and circuit boards were bursting out of the top of it. Beside it lay a couple of arms and legs. A pair of eyes sat in a dish.

'The best glass eyes there are on the market,' said Kruschke. 'None of the plastic rubbish that you see everywhere. And look at this.' He pointed to a leg. 'Silicone. Lifelike. You can see the veins shining through. Even varicose veins, if necessary.'

He tittered and took a bunch of keys out of his pocket. He opened the door of a closet. Inside was a woman's headless body. He picked up the head from the table and placed it carefully onto the body. Then he took a brown wig from a stand and draped it over the head. Then he tweaked the hair into place, murmuring, 'Now you're pretty again, my girl. But not just that. Do you notice how feelings are streaming through your body? Joy and pain, happiness and puzzlement, love and hate. And to whom do you owe it all? To me. Your creator.'

The children looked at each other. The man was mad. He had to be mad. Bruno cleared his throat, embarrassed.

Kruschke turned around. 'This is Sarah. Isn't she lovely?' He stroked her cheek. 'And so clever. She knows everything there is to know. There is nothing that she can't tell you. Give it a try. Ask something.'

He picked up a remote control that was no bigger than a matchbox and pressed a button.

Sarah opened her eyes. 'I know everything. I am so clever,' she twittered.

'When and how did Muhammad Ali gain his world title back?' asked Bruno.

'On the third of October 1974, in the last minute of the eighth round, Muhammad Ali knocked George Foreman out with two quick left-right combinations.'

'Whooo! That's right!' cried Bruno. 'That was some fight, I can tell you.'

Sophie threw her eyes up.

'Anything else you'd like to know?' asked Kruschke.

'Where is my mother?' asked Emily.

'A mother is the complement of a screw, otherwise known as a nut. There are four-way nuts, pipe nuts, ring nuts, knurled nuts, wing nuts –'

'Shut up!' shouted Emily. 'I'm not talking about some kind of screw. I want to know where my mother is.'

'Hooded nuts, beetle nuts, flanged nuts ...' Sarah went on calmly, until Kruschke silenced her at the press of a button.

'I'm sure your mother is having her supper with the others,' said Kruschke. 'Let's go and see.'

He opened another door that led into a dusty passageway. It brought them to the former factory floor, where Vibke Paulsen was just setting the tables. Nicholas was putting out the cutlery.

'Where on earth have you been, Kruschke?' she asked indignantly. 'All hell has broken loose here.'

'What's happened?'

'Wohlfarth's mother has risen from the dead,' said Vibke Paulsen.

'Are our mothers not here?' asked Emily.

'No, of course not. I thought they were with Kruschke.' Vibke Paulsen seemed puzzled.

Ramona Bottle came running into the room. 'The school is closing down,' she gasped. 'We're all being let go.'

Sven-Ole came in after her. 'What a shame! I've lost interest in sheep. This job was pretty good.'

'Where are our mothers?' screeched Emily.

'Well, they're with Kruschke ...' Sven-Ole turned around.

'Where is he? He was here just a minute ago.'

'We have to find him,' cried Emily. 'He's done something to them.'

'Kruschke?' Vibke Paulsen shook her head. 'Not him. He wouldn't hurt a fly.'

'All he cares about are his dolls,' Sven-Ole added. 'But don't worry, I'll find your mothers. They can't be far away.'

But Emily was already out the door and on the way to the warehouse. Sophie and Bruno ran after her.

'Wait up!' called Bruno. 'What can Kruschke have done? One man against seventeen women? How could that ...'

But Emily wasn't listening. She was running along by the shelves. She stumbled on a teddy that had fallen to the floor, grabbed hold of a pile of palettes to steady herself and saw a pair of trouser-legs disappearing behind a shelf.

'There he is!' she called to Bruno and Sophie.

Kruschke was running towards the curtained-off area where he kept his Annas. With one swift movement, he yanked the plastic curtain aside.

'Stop!' yelled Emily. 'Stay right where you are!'

But Kruschke took no notice of her. He disappeared in behind his dolls. The children heard a rattling, followed by a metallic click. And then they came marching out, eleven smiling Aunt Annas, all dolled up in their pale blue cardigans ... and every single one of them had a revolver in her hand.

Chapter 21

The mothers were really getting to know what fear felt like. The water was rising faster and faster now. They tried to get away from it, but behind them was nothing but a bare concrete wall. They were huddling now with their knees pulled up. Their trouser legs or skirts were wringing wet. Some of the candles had already gone out. It was getting darker; darker and colder.

'When does the tide reach its highest point?' asked Sophie's mother.

'Haven't a clue,' said Susie. 'Yesterday morning I had no trouble going around the end of the fence without getting my feet wet, but then by afternoon I couldn't do that any more.

'Is it not always twelve hours between low and high tide?' asked Clingy Mum and then gave a yelp as cold water sloshed into her shoes.

'The question is, how high does the water come in this bunker?' said Earth Mother. 'Maybe it will only come up as high as our waists.'

Sophie's mother took a candle and held it close to the concrete wall. Then she groaned. 'The watermark is almost as high as the ceiling. You can see by the dark colouration.' She fingered the mark on the wall. 'And feel it,' she added. 'It's damp here still since the last high tide.'

'But that means we're going to drown!' said Clingy Mum in astonishment.

'Ah, rubbish,' said Bruno's mother. 'They must have missed us long ago.'

'They'll be looking for us by now,' said Earth Mother.

'But nobody knows where we are,' said Susie. 'Except Kruschke. And he's not going to tell anyone.'

'My goodness, that man has a screw loose all right,' said Sophie's mother and tapped her temple to show that she thought Snivelling Susie had a screw loose too. 'But I still think he's harmless. You're jumping to conclusions.'

'Exactly,' someone else agreed. 'He told us to be careful because the door gets stuck. The wind must have banged it shut.'

'No door sticks so badly that it can't be opened by the combined strength of seventeen women,' said Susie. 'I'm sure Kruschke locked us in.'

'Why would he do that?' asked Earth Mother. 'What good would that do him?'

'I wish I knew,' said Susie.

❉

Emily rubbed her eyes. What she was looking at was like a scene out of a film, a film she would never have chosen to watch. There stood eleven Aunt Annas with revolvers, every one of them pointed at her. And not only at her but at Sophie and Bruno and at Vibke Paulsen, Nicholas and Ramona Bottle, who had arrived in response to Emily's horrified scream.

Kruschke had set himself up in front of his creations. His left eye was wandering from one to the other, while his right eye stared straight ahead.

'If you don't all disappear from here right now, there could be an accident,' he said menacingly.

'Hell's bells, Kruschke, what is this all about?' asked Vibke Paulsen. 'You don't really mean it, do you?'

'I absolutely do mean it.'

The 'tock, tock' of a walking stick could be heard. Frau Wohlfarth was coming down the stairs. Behind her, with his head uncharacteristically ducked, came her son, carrying Henry the Fourth.

On seeing the old woman, Kruschke backed up a bit.

'Kruschke, you are an idiot!' she yelled at him. 'And you always were. My husband should have thrown you out back then when you torched half the factory.'

Kruschke touched his right eye. 'That's when I lost my eye. All because that old skinflint used cheap gunpowder from China in his cartridges.'

'Stuff and nonsense! My husband received several awards for his inventions in the field of rapid-fire munitions.'

'*His* inventions. You must be joking!' screeched Kruschke. 'I invented all those things!'

'Bah,' Frau Wohlfarth said dismissively.

'Kruschke really wasn't to blame for the explosion, Mother,' Wohlfarth dared to interrupt.

'Silence! You have nothing to add to this conversation,' said the old woman, pointing her stick at Kruschke. 'If anyone is going to disappear from here it will be you. You and your dollies.' She pointed at the Annas. 'As far as I am concerned, you and your Annas can go to hell.'

Kruschke stepped right up to the old lady.

'I have spent my whole life being ordered around by people

like you. First by your husband, then by your son. But that's all over now.'

He pressed a button on his remote control, and the Annas stepped forward, put their revolver hands out and scrunched up their eyes, as if to concentrate on their targets.

Kruschke's voice became high and shrill. 'In future, there will be no more people like you. Because my dolls will revolutionise the world.'

The children shrank back. Ramona Bottle got hold of Vibke Paulsen. Nicholas was hiding behind Sophie.

'You and your stupid mother school,' spat Kruschke, looking at Wohlfarth. 'Surely you don't think you can really make good mothers out of these idle, stupid, irresponsible women. My Annas, on the other hand, are perfect. They have an unlimited capacity to learn. And one day they will be able to reproduce themselves and then finally the world will be the way I imagine it.'

'He's nuts,' whispered Vibke Paulsen. 'He was always a bit odd, but now …'

Sophie took a deep breath and took a step towards Kruschke. 'Perfect, my eye! Our Aunt Anna was just weird. She gave Nicholas cat food. And she scared him. I want to see my mother – right now!'

'Me too,' said Emily.

'Me too,' said Bruno.

Kruschke gave an evil laugh. 'You want to see your mothers? Well, I am sorry to inform you that that will not be possible.' He checked his watch. 'They should be just about up to their necks in it by now, as the saying goes.'

Beside himself, Wohlfarth yelled, 'What have you done with my students?'

'I never touched them,' said Kruschke. 'Like all women, they are curious. I can't help it if they want to go sticking their noses into things that do not concern them.'

'What's that supposed to mean?' asked Vibke Paulsen. And then, suddenly suspecting the worst, she shouted, 'Not … not the bunker?'

'Oh, God!' cried Ramona Bottle, clapping her hand to her mouth.

Emily looked at her, her eyes wide with terror.

'What does that mean?' she asked.

But nobody took the slightest bit of notice of her.

'We have to call the coastguard,' called Wohlfarth, running to an old-fashioned telephone hanging on the wall.

Kruschke pressed another button on his remote. A shot rang out. It sounded like an explosion in the huge building.

Wohlfarth stood stock-still. He stared blankly down at Henry the Fourth, whom he was still carrying in his arms. The sleeve of Wohlfarth's jacket had a neat hole in it. Henry had been hit.

'My poor Henry!' cried Frau Wohlfarth.

The bullet hadn't hurt Henry, but it had shot his topnotch clean off.

'Get away from that telephone!' Kruschke ordered. 'As you see, these ladies are good shots.'

While Kruschke's eyes were on Wohlfarth, Bruno tried to reach the outside pocket of his rucksack, which he was carrying over his shoulder.

'We must do something!' screamed Ramona Bottle, in a total panic.

Kruschke swung around. 'One more word out of you and …'

He pressed a button on the remote and one of the Annas stepped right up to Ramona Bottle and pressed a revolver against her chest with a smile.

'Look, have a bit of sense, Kruschke,' called Vibke Paulsen, who was able to think practically, even in a situation like this.

Kruschke laughed again. 'Me? I'm not shooting anyone here. Regrettable programming error. These things happen.'

'We're witnesses that you …' Ramona Bottle started.

But Kruschke would not let her say any more. 'There will be no witnesses here because I am going to bring this business to an end right now.'

He was just about to press another button when something very strange happened. Still smiling sweetly, the Annas dropped their revolvers and started to form a circle.

Kruschke turned on Bruno and grabbed the remote control out of his hand.

'You can forget about that, my boy.'

'Yeah, sure,' said Bruno, landing a right hook on Kruschke's nose so hard that he hurt his hand.

After that, everything happened at once. Kruschke fell to the ground, old Frau Wohlfarth started lashing out with her stick at the Annas who were encircling her, battering them into bits, Bruno was wringing his sore hand, Henry the Fourth piddled on Wohlfarth's arm with the shock of it all and Vibke Paulsen yelled, after one look at Kruschke, 'He's passed out. Water, quick!'

Ramona Bottle said, 'Serves him right!'

Vibke Paulsen made a not very polite gesture and said, 'But he has to tell us what he has done with the mothers.'

She ran off and came back with a bucket of water, which she threw in Kruschke's face. He spluttered and spat and opened first his real and then his artificial eye. 'Sarah,' he murmured. 'Sarah, where are you?'

By now, Wohlfarth had got rid of the dog and was screaming into the phone. 'What? No, that can't ... we need help immediately! Yes, I understand, but please, hurry!'

He hung up. 'The lifeboat can't be put out to sea. Engine trouble. They won't be here for at least two hours.'

'What time is it now?' asked Vibke Paulsen.

'It is exactly nineteen thirty-seven Central European Summer Time,' said a monotone voice. A woman in a flowery dress was coming out of Kruschke's workshop.

'Prototype 3131!' cried Wohlfarth. 'I thought she had drowned.'

The woman came closer and stopped beside Kruschke.

'Help me, Sarah,' called Kruschke. 'Pass me that revolver there.'

And before anyone could do anything about it, Sarah had bent down and picked up one of the revolvers.

'Give it to me!' Kruschke sat up. 'Remember what I taught you,' he admonished her.

'I love you. You are a handsome man. I love you. You are a handsome man. I love –'

'Give it to me!' cried Kruschke.

Sarah stretched out her hand. 'Here you are,' she said politely and bashed him over the head with the gun. Kruschke hit the floor for the second time.

At that moment, Sven-Ole came bursting into the hall. 'I've looked everywhere, the whole beach, the dunes – nothing,' he managed to get out between gasps.

'They're probably in the bunker,' said Vibke Paulsen tonelessly, 'and it is filling right up with water.'

Sven-Ole's eyes opened wide in horror. 'Oh Lord God! What a –'

'Bunkers are defended structures which are supposed to protect those who are inside them from the effects of weapons. They are usually built of concrete or steel,' Sarah rattled off.

'Shut up, you stupid doll!' called Frau Wohlfarth, raising her stick.

Bruno threw himself across the old woman's body. 'Stop! Wait a minute!'

He turned towards Sarah. 'What do you know about the bunker on Nordfall?'

'The bunker on Nordfall was built during World War II and was intended as an observation point from which enemy ships could be seen. There is an underground passage from it to the only guesthouse on the island, through which alcohol was frequently smuggled, and –'

'The secret passage! Of course!' Vibke Paulsen smacked her forehead. 'Why didn't I think of it! Come on, we have to get to Dune View!'

'And what about Kruschke?' asked Ramona Bottle.

'I love you. You are a handsome man,' twittered Sarah again. But Kruschke couldn't hear her. He was lying unconscious among the remains of his dolls.

'He's out of action anyway,' said Bruno. 'My finger too, unfortunately.' He held up his right hand, the one he had used to biff Kruschke. His little finger was hanging at an alarming angle.

'Henry and I will personally guard this gentleman,' said Frau Wohlfarth, poking Kruschke in the stomach. 'And you can stay here and clean up this mess, Walther,' she ordered her son, pointing at the scattered arms and legs of the destroyed Annas.

'I'll help him,' said Ramona Bottle, giving Wohlfarth an encouraging look, but he had eyes only for his mother and said, 'Yes, Mother; certainly, Mother.'

Vibke Paulsen and Sven-Ole were out of earshot by now. They were running out of the hall with the children.

Lührsen, the owner of Dune View, was more than a little surprised when the door to his bar was flung open and Vibke Paulsen came running up to him, her chest heaving.

'Well, Vibke, has your husband run out of beer or what?' he asked.

'Have you got the key to the underground passage?' she cried. 'Our students are trapped in the bunker.'

Hinnerk, who had been sitting at one of the tables, jumped up. 'What are you lot doing here again?'

'Stop asking questions, just come with us into the cellar,' said the guesthouse owner. 'You too, Sven-Ole. We need strong men.'

'What about that fellow?' asked Vibke Paulsen pointing at a half-collapsed figure in the corner, with a peaked cap pulled over his face.

'He's the one who stole my ice cream!' cried Nicholas. 'And he threw my Mousie in the bin.'

'That's Alfred,' said Bruno.

'And who is Alfred when he's at home?' asked Vibke Paulsen.

'Frau Wohlfarth's butler,' said Bruno.

'Frau Wohlfarth's chauffeur,' said Sophie.

'Frau Wohlfarth's sea-captain,' said Emily.

'Well, whatever else he is,' said the guesthouse keeper, 'at the moment he is only one thing, and that is dead drunk. First he drank tea. Then tea with rum. Then just rum.'

'I could do with something myself to give me a bit of strength,' said Vibke Paulsen. 'My poor nerves! Bring me an egg-nog, Swantje. And a hot chocolate for the little lad.'

There was a trapdoor behind the counter, which Lührsen was opening. A narrow staircase was revealed. In the brightly lit cellar there were beer barrels, crates and all sorts of stuff. They went through a door into a narrow hallway with shelves full of bottles at the end of it.

'Now what?' asked Sven-Ole.

'Help me to push the shelves away. My grandfather put them here as camouflage. The passageway to the bunker is behind them.'

'So it's true that drink used to be smuggled?' asked Sophie.

The guesthouse keeper shrugged his shoulders. He was carefully removing bottles. 'That was a long time ago,' he growled.

A bottle clattered to the floor and smashed.

'Watch out!' he snapped at Bruno. 'That was a 1969 Bordeaux.'

'To hell with your stupid wine,' said Bruno. 'Our mothers are drowning!'

❇

They weren't drowning just yet, but the water had reached nearly as high as their bottoms. Only one of the candles was still burning, but its light was getting weaker by the minute.

'I should have been nicer to her,' Sophie's mother was wailing. 'A girl who is going through puberty needs understanding and love; I know that now. I preferred Nicholas, because he is so much easier to look after.'

'Don't blame yourself,' said Susie. 'I think children know very well that they are loved, no matter how badly you behave.'

'Well, ours don't seem to have known it. Otherwise, why would they write such horrible things about us?' said Earth Mother bitterly.

'Did you never complain about your mother?' asked Susie.

Of course they had. They all had stories to tell about the dreadful mothers they'd had.

'Mine said, at a school party, loud enough for everyone to hear, that I shouldn't have any bean salad, because it would make me fart,' said Clingy Mum.

'Oh, God!' said everyone in unison, and the women forgot their present troubles in remembering hurts from the past. But not for long. Then the moaning started up again.

'My panties are wet through.'

'I'm freezing.'

'When is someone going to get us out of here?'

'How could they?' asked Susie. 'The entrance to the bunker is in the sea by now.'

'They'll have to get divers,' said Sophie's mother.

'That's a great idea, Mrs Supersmart,' said Bruno's mother

dismissively. 'Maybe they could get in here, but how would they get us out? I never thought of bringing my diving suit. Did you?'

'Well, it'd be hard to find one to fit you, anyway,' retorted Sophie's mother.

'You stupid –'

'Oh, stop squabbling,' said Susie. 'That's not going to get us anywhere. I wonder if there is another way out.'

She took hold of the last candle and went feeling her way along the back wall of the bunker. Her fingers moved over slithery moss until they came to a rusty bar.

'There's something here!' she called. 'A ladder.'

❀

The passageway that led from Dune View to the bunker was low and narrow. Not even Emily, who was the smallest, was able to walk standing up straight. But mostly it was dark. Hinnerk did have a torch, but its light only reached a few yards.

They struggled on, bent over. A rat brushed past Emily and she gave a muffled screech. But then she heard something.

'Psst!' she went. 'Can you hear that?'

They all stopped and listened. The sound was quite clear now. Knocking.

❀

Susie was standing at the top of the ladder and was hammering on the wooden hatch behind it. She finally gave up and climbed back down. Down into the water that was now chest-high on her.

'Let me have a go!' said Sophie's mother.

She clambered up and banged with her fist on the slimy wood, until she slipped.

'Oh, give over with this nonsense,' said Earth Mother. 'Who could possibly hear us?'

The water was up to her waist by now. And she was the tallest.

Clingy Mum was gasping for air. 'I want to get out! Let me get on the ladder.'

'No, me!' called another.

And another one spluttered desperately, 'I've swallowed water, I'm drowning!'

All the mothers gathered around the ladder and tried to pull Sophie's mother down off it. She cried, 'Shut up! I hear something. Someone is there!'

'You're lying,' shouted Fitness Mum. 'You just want to stay up there, where it's safe. Get down here!'

At that very moment, the hatch over their heads opened.

'Hang on, Mum,' called Sophie, holding out a hand to her mother. 'I'll get you out of here.'

Wet through and rather emotional, all the mothers started climbing, one after another, up the ladder and through the narrow opening into the passageway.

Sophie's mother didn't want to let go of her daughter. 'My angel, my darling! You saved us! Good heavens, I'm afraid even to think about what might have happened. Are you all right? What have you done with your hair? It looks terrible.' And then finally she asked, 'Where is Nicholas?'

'Vibke Paulsen is looking after him,' Sophie assured her. 'And my hair looks the same as it always does.'

Susie sneezed several times. Emily gave her a hanky.

'I was afraid you had believed my lie,' snuffled Susie. 'Kruschke made me do it. Otherwise he said he wouldn't pull you out of the water that day.'

'You were crying when you said goodbye to me,' said Emily. 'That struck me as odd. You never cry.'

Susie laughed, and then she sneezed again. 'You must be joking. Do you know what they call me here? Snivelling Susie!'

'No dilly-dallying there at the back!' called Sven-Ole. 'It's high time everyone was on dry land. Oh, yes, by the way, do you know this one? A blonde comes to a tunnel ...'

'We know it!' came several voices at once, and he shut up.

A little while later they were all sitting around in Dune View, wrapped in blankets, drinking hot tea or something stronger, all gabbling away at the same time.

Lührsen hadn't seen his bar this full for years. Sven-Ole had run to the factory to bring the news to Wohlfarth that all the mothers were safe. Alfred, who was not yet quite sober, had insisted on accompanying him.

'Ma ... Ma ... Madam will be ... be ... be needing me, for sure,' he'd babbled. 'And I ha ... ha ... haven't drunk anything.'

Pleased as Punch, Nicholas sat up on Sophie's lap, like a king on his throne. 'You saved everyone, Sofa, didn't you?'

'It was really Bruno,' said Sophie. 'If he hadn't asked Kruschke's Sarah about the bunker, we'd never have found out about the secret passage.'

'Well, actually, it might have occurred to me eventually,' said Vibke Paulsen sheepishly.

'Strictly speaking,' said Bruno, 'we have Emily to thank for it all. If she hadn't insisted that we should go looking for old Frau Wohlfarth, we'd never have come back to Nordfall at all.'

'Oh, dear, I can't bear to think about it,' said Clingy Mum.

'All three of you rescued us,' said Susie. 'We can all be really proud of our children, can't we?'

Sophie's and Bruno's mothers nodded. The other fourteen looked a bit embarrassed.

'I just hope my Nadine will be pleased to see me tomorrow,' said Suspicious Mum. 'She's probably spent the whole time in front of the TV.'

'My Timmy has probably got used to sleeping alone,' wailed Clingy Mum. 'Or, worse still, maybe he sleeps with that robot woman.'

'You think you have problems?' said Bruno's mother. 'I really have something to worry about.'

'What's that?' asked Sophie's mother.

'Whether we are ever going to get anything to eat, since our picnic fell through.'

'Have we got any tinned beef stew, Swantje?' Lührsen asked his waitress, who was standing near Hinnerk and listening as he told how he had, at great danger to himself, pulled seventeen women out of the water.

She threw a languorous look at him, then she said to Lührsen, 'At least ten tins.'

'Good, well then, pour the lot into a pot, add onions, peppers, tomato purée and a couple of bay leaves, and in ten minutes we'll have goulash soup.

Nobody could ever remember having eaten such good soup. Even Earth Mother managed to forget, in the face of the steaming and fragrant soup, that she was a vegetarian. That feeling of well-being that you only get from having lived through a shared danger gradually spread through them all.

Bruno's mother licked her lips with satisfaction and smiled proudly. It was, after all, her son who had knocked Kruschke out.

Bruno plucked up the courage to say, 'I don't think I can ever play the piano again, Mum.' He held up the little finger of his right hand. 'It's broken.'

'Oh, Bruno, that doesn't matter one little bit. Forget the stupid piano. I have wonderful news for you: not only may you box, you absolutely must! A talent like yours is a rare thing.'

Bruno wasn't sure whether he should be pleased about this change of heart or not.

Then Susie asked, 'So what's the story with Kruschke anyway? Has he been locked up? He did try to kill us, after all.'

'Wohlfarth's mother is guarding him,' said Emily. 'And that's worse than jail.'

❋

As the mothers were leaving Dune View later that evening, the wind was blowing hard. The sea was battering the jetty fiercely. New breakers kept rolling in and crashing onto the beach.

'I wouldn't like to be out there just now,' said Sophie with a shudder.

'You mean, *I* wouldn't,' said Bruno, who was feeling ill even at the thought of having to take the boat back to the mainland.

'It'll have calmed down by tomorrow,' said Emily.

They were planning to spend the night in the WIMI and then catch the ferry home in the morning.

An eerie stillness greeted them when they came into the factory.

'Where are they all, then?' asked Vibke Paulsen.

Kruschke was nowhere to be seen. The remains of the dolls

were still lying around on the floor, and a walking stick lay near by.

'Something has happened,' said Emily, running up the steps to Wohlfarth's office.

Wohlfarth sat slumped on a chair. Ramona Bottle stood next to him, her hand on his shoulder. Sven-Ole had a glass in his hand and was trying to get away from Henry the Fourth, who was hanging on with his teeth to Sven-Ole's trouser-leg. On a sofa, pale and with her eyes closed, lay old Frau Wohlfarth. Alfred, still swaying slightly, was bent over her, fanning her face.

'Where's Kruschke?' asked Susie, who had followed the children.

'He's done a runner,' said Sven-Ole. 'When he regained consciousness, he got hold of the walking stick and smacked the old lady one on the noggin with it. Then he upped and left with his doll. Let go, you mucky little beast!' He shook his leg and the Pekinese finally let go of his trouser-leg.

'Kruschke won't get far,' said Wohlfarth. 'The coastguard has arrived and they've gone after his boat.'

'She's opening her eyes,' said Alfred and bent again over his mistress. 'Are you feeling better, Madam?'

Old Frau Wohlfarth sat up. 'Alfred! You've been drinking! I can smell it.'

The phone on Wohlfarth's desk rang. He picked it up. 'Yes, yes. Understood. Oh dear, well then, there's nothing to be done.' He hung up. 'Kruschke's boat has disappeared without trace. In those seas, it has very likely capsized.'

Wohlfarth looked at Susie and raised his arms helplessly. 'I didn't plan for any of this to happen. You have to believe me. All I wanted was to make children happy. First with my toys, and then by trying to turn bad mothers into better ones.' He sighed. 'But I made a mess of it.'

'As usual, boy,' said Frau Wohlfarth, who by now was standing, supported by Alfred (or perhaps it was Alfred who was supported by her) in front of her son. 'Failed again.'

'You wanted to make children happy because you had an unhappy childhood yourself, isn't that right?' said Susie softly.

Wohlfarth nodded, and a tear fell on the pile of questionnaires.

'Poppycock! You lacked for nothing,' said his mother.

'Not true,' said Wohlfarth. 'I lacked the most important thing. Love.'

'Love!' spat the old woman contemptuously. 'Love is for softies.'

'There is one thing I don't understand,' said Bruno. 'Why did you pretend your mother was dead?'

'And why did you say she was the best mother in the world?' said Emily.

'Which she clearly is not,' added Sophie.

'I wanted my mother to be proud of me,' said Wohlfarth quietly. 'That's why I made up all that stuff about the bank in New York. And so that people wouldn't think it odd that she never came to see me, I told everyone on Nordfall that she was dead.'

He turned to the portrait of his mother. 'I had that picture painted from a photo. I had to pay the painter extra because it took him so long to make her smile. And then I tried to imagine how my childhood might have been and I wrote it all up in my diary. A childhood with a mother who was loving, warm, clever and full of humour. And one who would always carry in her locket …' at this, he pointed at the gold medallion that the woman in the picture was wearing, 'a lock of my baby hair.' He gave a sob.

'And what is really in it?' Emily wanted to know.

'Well, let's see,' said the old woman, opening the locket. A dirty grey clump of something was revealed, with a straggle of blue ribbon around it. 'Henry the First's topnotch, of course.'

Chapter 22

The next morning, the storm was over. Woolly white clouds drifted across a blue sky. The sands gleamed yellow. The fields and meadows were a soft green.

Wohlfarth's school for mothers was like a youth hostel where a visiting class was getting ready to go home. All animosity, quarrels, dramas big and small, had been forgotten. They were all united by the feeling of having survived a great challenge. On top of that was a mixture of sadness at parting and gladness at the thought of going home at last.

Suspicious Mum, who was checking all the lockers and cupboards to make sure no one had stolen her hairbrush, said, 'I swear to God, I will never read my daughter's diary again. Except in an emergency, of course.'

Another mother was vowing to let her eleven-year-old son cycle to school, all by himself.

But Clingy Mum could only shake her head. 'No, no. I will still take Timmy to school. But I'll let him go into the classroom by himself.'

They were outdoing each other in good intentions as they left the factory in high good spirits.

Vibke Paulsen, Ramona Bottle and Sven-Ole were at the gate, waiting to take leave of their students.

'But where is Herr Wohlfarth?' asked Sophie's mother.

Red-eyed, Ramona Bottle was blowing her nose. 'His mother took him to Hamburg early this morning,' she sniffled. 'And she said she wouldn't let him out of her sight for a minute, because he would be sure to get up to some mischief.'

'That woman really is a dragon,' said Vibke Paulsen. 'I liked her better when she was dead.'

'That reminds me,' said Sven-Ole. 'What happens if you laugh yourself half to death twice?'

'In future, you'll have to tell your jokes to someone else,' said Vibke Paulsen. 'None of us will miss them, that's for sure.'

Susie took Ramona Bottle aside and said, 'This is your chance, Ramona. Go to Hamburg and rescue him from the clutches of that woman. He will be eternally grateful to you.'

'Do you really think so?'

Susie nodded. 'I really think so. I may not have been a good student, and maybe I will never make a good mother, but I understand people. Well, goodbye now.'

And the mothers left for the jetty.

'Do you think I should go to him?' said Ramona Bottle after the mothers had gone. 'Do you think he needs me?'

'Follow your heart,' said Vibke Paulsen.

Ramona didn't need telling a second time. She grabbed hold of a bike that was leaning against a wall and sped off in the direction of the harbour, her tyres squeaking, calling, 'Walther, I'm on my way!'

Lührsen, Swantje and Hinnerk were standing outside Dune View, watching the chattering gaggle of women marching to the jetty.

'Well, whatever sort of a place that WIMI was,' said the guesthouse owner, 'it's a pity it doesn't exist any more. Who's going to eat my food now?'

Hinnerk nodded in agreement. 'It's terrible. I caught a couple of fine fat fish this morning and all.'

The ferry from the mainland docked on the island, and no sooner had the ferryman thrown out the mooring rope than a horde of camera-bedecked men disembarked, pushed the mothers aside and started running towards Dune View.

'Who the dickens are they?' asked Swantje, astonished.

'Reporters,' said Lührsen. He knew a thing or two.

A reporter had shoved a microphone under his nose.

'So, what do locals have to say about how you've been living for years with a murderer?'

'What murderer?' asked Swantje, bemused.

'He's wanted,' said another, fiddling about with his camera.

'We heard it on the police radio channel. Someone on Nordfall has been farming artificial people, and apparently he drowned seventeen women in an old World War Two bunker.'

The guesthouse owner pointed to the ferry, which was just moving away from the harbour, tooting loudly.

The mothers were waving from the deck, and Hinnerk waved back.

'Those are the women who are supposed to have been murdered,' he said. 'Hale and hearty.'

'But that's thanks to my Hinnerk here,' said Swantje proudly. 'He saved them from drowning just in the nick of time.' She continued, even though her boss shot her a warning look. 'There's a secret passage from our place to the bunker.'

A fat, sweating man pushed his way forward. 'Could I see it?'

'Me too!' cried the others.

'Stop, stop!' Lührsen cried, spreading his arms defensively.

'Only three people can visit the tunnel at a time. And it costs fifty euro a head. Lunch is included, but drinks are extra. A guided tour of the factory, in which the remains of the robots are to be seen, can also be arranged.'

Money was immediately produced, and the mob pushed its way into the bar.

Hinnerk grinned at Swantje. 'I'll buy you a Coke this evening,' he promised. 'I think there will be takers for my fish after all.'

❋

The voyage back to the mainland was almost disappointingly uneventful.

Bruno sat beside his mother. She asked him excitedly, 'Do you know what day it is today?'

'Yes, of course. It's the nineteenth of June. Why do you ask?'

'Because today is a special day, a historic date,' Bruno's mother crowed.

'Because we're going home, you mean?'

'No, darling. On the nineteenth of June 1936, Max Schmeling knocked out his opponent, Joe Louis, in the second round. This is how …'

She told him the whole story of the boxing match in such detail, and she made it sound so exciting, that for the first time ever he was not seasick on a boat.

Emily and her mother did not say much to each other during the crossing. They had said most of what they had to say during the night, and now they just watched the seagulls that were following the ferry.

'I wish I could have a holiday here with you,' Susie said. 'But without having to go to school, of course.'

'Do you know what?' said Emily. 'I'd rather we went to the mountains for our holiday. I've had enough of the sea.'

Nicholas and Sophie were standing at the railing, feeding the seagulls with the bread rolls Vibke Paulsen had packed for their lunch.

'It's just as well I went away,' said Sophie's mother to Bruno's mother. 'Those two have totally changed. They're the best of friends.'

But just then, Sophie suddenly screeched, 'Put that thing down! Get rid of it right now!'

Nicholas crowed, 'It's going to bite you. It's going to pinch you on the nose.' He was waving a dead crab in her face.

'I suppose it was too good to be true,' said Sophie's mother with a sigh.

'I'm dying to hear what my husband will say when he finds out he has been living with a doll for days,' Bruno's mother speculated. 'Typical man, doesn't take a bit of notice as long as his dinner is on the table every evening.'

'You're lucky,' said Clingy Mum. 'Your aunts are gone. We still have to get rid of ours.'

'Just show them the door,' said Bruno. 'Or you could keep them. They are great cleaners.'

'But they're useless at reading stories,' Nicholas chipped in.

'Mummy will read to you now,' his mother said to him.

Nicholas shook his head.

'No, Sofa will read to me. She's much better at it than you.'

Sophie's mother smiled a bitter little smile. 'I seem to be quite superfluous.'

'That's right,' said Sophie. 'We got on just fine without you.'

But then she elbowed her mother in the ribs. 'I'm glad you're coming home all the same. I had nobody to fight with.'

When they got to Südersiel it was time to say goodbye. Some of them boarded the train. Others got into their cars.

Susie offered to drive Sophie, Nicholas and their mother to Hamburg.

But when she saw the tiny, rusty car with its bashed-in door, Sophie's mother shook her head. 'No, thanks; it would be a bit tight. We'll go with Earth Mother. She has a Land Rover. There's more room.'

'Oh, very green, a car like that,' said Bruno who was just saying goodbye to Sophie and Emily.

'How are we going to keep in touch?' asked Emily.

'We can email each other,' said Sophie.

'I have a better idea,' said Bruno. 'We can use Wohlfarth's website. You know, www.worldsworstmothers.eek. He doesn't need it any more. We can use the message board and we can all keep in touch that way.'

'We'll never know now which of us would have won first prize.'

'How do you mean, first prize?' asked Emily.

'The one with the world's worst mother was supposed to win a four-week, mother-free holiday on an island.'

'Oh, yes, I'd forgotten,' said Emily.

'Well, only one person could win that prize,' said Bruno, 'and that is Wohlfarth himself.'

'I wonder what will become of him,' said Emily. 'Maybe he

will move back into his old room at home and get shouted at every day.'

'Yes, and he'll have to brush Henry the Fourth's hair.'

'I'm much more concerned about what is going to become of us,' said Bruno. 'I'd also like to know if Wohlfarth has actually managed to improve our mothers.'

'Come on, Bruno!' called his mother. 'Our train is leaving any minute.'

Bruno gave Sophie his hand and she shook it vigorously.

'Ouch!' cried Bruno suddenly. 'My finger!'

'Oh, I'm sorry,' said Sophie. 'I just wanted to say thanks, because … well, if it hadn't been for you, Bruno, there'd have been a catastrophe.'

'You're a good boxer,' said Nicholas. 'I have a present for you.'

He pulled the dead crab carefully out of his pocket. He was missing a claw, and he didn't smell too good.

'Thank you, Nicholas,' said Bruno, taking the crab. 'It will remind me of you.'

Then Sophie and Nicholas and their mother got into Earth Mother's big car, and off they sped.

Bruno waved at Sophie one last time and then went with his mother to the railway station.

Susie got into the driver's seat of her little car, and Emily tried, in vain, to open the passenger door. It was still stuck, naturally. At last she managed it and almost fell on her bottom.

'I'll have it fixed tomorrow,' said her mother, when Emily was in the car at last. 'I promise.'

'As long as we have enough petrol,' said Emily.

Her mother turned on the engine and checked the petrol gauge.

'No worries. We have enough to get home and back, twice.'

They got twenty kilometres before the car stopped in the middle of the road. Luckily, a farmer on a tractor came trundling by and towed the car to the next petrol station.

'I don't think the school for mothers did me much good,' said Susie miserably.

'You're dead right,' said Emily, and then she started to laugh.

Chapter 23

www.worldsworstmothers.eek

21 June
Hey, Sophie and Emily, how's it going?

We got home in one piece, and my father looked pretty cheesed off when my mother told him he'd been taken in by a robot! Claimed he'd always thought this Aunt Anna was a bit strange, but since he has always found my mother's family impossible (especially Great-aunt Adelheid with her stupid viola), he didn't think anything of it.

Bruno

PS: Sophie, you can tell Nicholas I had to bury the crab in the garden, it just stank too much.

1 July
Dear Bruno,

Our trip home was anything but good. My mother ran out of petrol – again! Typical. The mother school doesn't seem to have done her any good. Yesterday, she was planning to cook a pizza for me and my friend for lunch. In the middle of it, it occurred to her that she had to pick up her shoes from the shoemaker. And while she was at the shoemaker's, she remembered that we were out of milk. When Charlotte and I arrived home from school, the fire brigade was at the door, because smoke was belching out of the kitchen window. Charlotte thought it was funny. I didn't.

But she did learn one thing: how to iron. She irons all the time. Even the towels. Can you believe it? Are you still boxing?

Emily

5 July

Hi, Emily

Am I still boxing? You'd better believe it! My mother has got it into her head that I am to be the next Muhammad Ali. I have to train every day, and she watches and tells me what I am doing wrong. Next week I have to go to a boxing camp, where they take it really seriously. I mean, I do like boxing, but it really gets on my wick the way my mother is so into it. I won't be online again until I get back. Fingers crossed I get through it without a black eye or a broken nose.

Have you heard from Sophie lately?

Enjoy the rest of the hols,

Bruno

17 July

Hey, there, everyone,

Couldn't write before, because we were on a cycling trip. Not at the North Sea, just along the River Elbe. My mother really took it badly when I told her I was going to have to repeat the year at school, but at least she didn't moan on about it.

That would nearly have been better than all these questions about how I am and whether I feel neglected. And she keeps following me around.

226

We didn't tell my stepfather that Aunt Anna was fake. My mother didn't want him to find out about the school for mothers. She was too embarrassed. The official story is that she went to one of those health farm places, and George says she looks really relaxed.

I have to go. Nicholas wants me to help him build a sandcastle. We have to do it while my mother is out, because otherwise she keeps banging on about how we have to dampen the sand and smooth the edges and all this stuff. 'I got an A in sandcastle building,' she says every time.

Best of luck!

Sophie

19 July

Hey, people, stumbled across this site. My mother was in this mother school too! But she hasn't improved much. She was only home when she sent Aunt Anna packing. After she looked after me so well the whole time. I think she was jealous, because I got on so well with her.

And, get this, she keeps reading my diary on the sly. Any ideas about how to make her stop? I'd be very glad to hear from you.

Nadine

21 July

Just write something that will make her realise you know she reads it. Then she'll be really embarrassed.

Best, Emily

23 July

Hi Emily,

That was a great idea. I wrote, 'Dear Mum, I know you are

reading this, and I find it totally mean. If you don't stop, I will tell Dad that your new dress was not a bargain at all, but cost 500 euro.' She swore she'd never read my diary again. But just to be sure, I bought one with a lock.

Enjoy what's left of the holidays,

Nadine

24 July

Hey everyone,

I just wanted to check who won the World's Worst Mothers competition. I took part in it, but I never heard another word. And now I see your mothers all went to this school for mothers. Can I send my mother there too?

Dragon Monster

Hey Dragon Monster,

Do you remember Chiara? We chatted before, but my name isn't really Chiara, it's Sophie. And I'm not fifteen, only thirteen.

The school for mothers doesn't exist any more. It's a long story.

Sophie

28 July

Hey everyone!

Guess who I saw today in a shop window on the Kudamm in Berlin? One of our Aunt Annas. I don't know which one, but I recognised her immediately, even though she had all this cool gear on instead of her stupid apron. Wonder what happened to the others? Let me know if you know anything.

Emily

28 July

I read in the newspaper today about a woman who was sent to a mental hospital because she kept on cleaning and cleaning. She stopped sleeping and eating. All she did was wash the floors. That has to be one of our 'ladies' who has just gone a bit too far; would you agree?

Sophie

29 July

Dear Emily, Dear Sophie,

I'm just back from boxing camp. Had to leave early, actually. The coach threw me out! Well, not me, really – my mother. She totally got on his nerves. She kept explaining the rules of boxing to him, and telling him that he wasn't doing enough for me, and that I am *so* talented.

Now she's looking for a new coach for me, only I've really gone off boxing altogether!

Mothers are such hard work!

Bruno

Howdy, folks!

We're called Jan and Jonas and we had an Aunt Anna too. She just went away. But we'd love to have her back. And our father is sad too that she's not here any more. He really liked her. Much better than he likes our mother, who cooks weird things that you really need to chew hard. With Aunt Anna, we always had sausages and hamburgers and kebabs. Our mother cooks sausages now too. They don't taste nice, but on the other hand they are good for you. But we don't want healthy sausages.

We want Aunt Anna!

Jan and Jonas

4 *August*

Dear Jan and Jonas,

You should be glad you are rid of Aunt Anna. She was fake, electronic, a robot! I know what I'm talking about.

All best, Bruno

Dear Bruno,

We don't care what Aunt Anna is, we just want her back. Any idea where we could buy another one? We're saving up.

Jan and Jonas

You haven't a hope. The fellow who built the Annas was drowned.

Bruno

Dear Emily, Sophie, Nicholas and Bruno,

I'm getting in touch like this because it's the easiest way and I have something to tell you. I don't know much about this Internet thingy, but Sven-Ole is typing this for me.

Walther Wohlfarth has come back! His mother died, for real this time. She was walking along by the Elbe with that awful Pekinese and he wanted to get together with a mongrel. Anyway, she went to separate them with her stick, lost her balance and fell into the water. It wouldn't have been so bad, because there happened to be a boat nearby that came to her aid, but she kept yelling so much at the mongrel's master and gulping water as she did so that they couldn't rescue her.

After the funeral, Wohlfarth came back to Nordfall, but he did not come alone. He has Ramona Bottle with him, that weird Alfred and … the dog. It seems that Henry the Fourth has inherited the mother's whole estate. I hope our boss isn't going to put up with that. I mean, you can't just cut your son off without a penny.

Nobody knows what he is planning. It's all a big secret.

Oh yes, and another thing – Sarah has turned up. Hinnerk fished her out of the water. She looked fine and the whole time she was warbling, 'I love you, you are a handsome man.' That's what Kruschke taught her, you remember. Hinnerk was charmed, because nobody had ever said anything like that to him before, but Swantje gave him such a hard time that in the end he sold Sarah to Lührsen. He's running these bunker tours now, and the doll tells the tourists all there is to know about the bunker and the secret passage. More and more trippers are coming to Nordfall every day. My husband has had to get new beach chairs. So Kruschke has brought us a bit of luck. There is no sign of him, by the way.

I hope your mothers are well, and you too. It really was a very exciting time that we had together.

Very best wishes from

Vibke Paulsen

PS And from me too, of course. I've ditched the stupid sheep, and now I am giving courses in sandcastle building. The tourists love it, and my jokes too, I might add. Do you know this one? How do you get a blonde to laugh on a Friday? You tell her a joke on Monday.

Keep well,

Sven-Ole

Ha ha ha. What a terrible joke! But thanks for getting in touch, Sven-Ole and Vibke Paulsen. That's mad about Wohlfarth, but we are not exactly grief-stricken, I have to say. And that fabulous villa in Blankenese now belongs to the stupid mutt. That's awful!

I'm great, by the way. My mother is totally back to normal. Only she doesn't nag me as much as she used to – now she lets Nicholas have it! He put a dead hedgehog in her bed recently, one he had scraped up off the road. It was half mummified, but its spines still prickled all the same. As you can imagine, my mother was not exactly over the moon about this.

The holidays are over now, which is sad, but my new class is fine. I still don't get maths, I have to admit. But Dragon Monster has promised to give me grinds. In exchange, I have to keep telling him all about our adventures on Nordfall. (If you are reading this, Julius, it's all true!)

Very best wishes,

from Sophie

(and of course from Nicholas too)

3 September

Hello all,

Listen, this mother-school business did do a bit of good. Wait till you hear the latest: my mother has taken up boxing! She just got so into it all that she started boxing herself. She's in training for her first contest this winter. My father was totally disgusted at first, but at this stage, he's come round and now he is quite proud of her! He even goes with her to her training sessions, to egg her on. I can hardly believe these are my parents. And the great thing is that my mother has no time now to be thinking about me and my talents. She isn't the slightest bit interested that I have taken up rowing.

Yes, that's right: I now get into a boat, of my own free will! What happened was, the cox in our school team wasn't available, so I said I'd give it a go. The weird thing is, I never get seasick when I'm doing it. So don't be surprised if you don't hear much from me, I'm really very busy these days.

    Bruno

Dear Bruno, Dear Sophie,

    I read something in the paper today that you will be interested in:

THE WORLD'S FIRST LUXURY HOTEL FOR DOGS OPENS ON NORDFALL
Walther Wohlfarth has given up his job as a creator of electronic toys
and has found a new career: a hotel for high-society dogs. Every dog
has its own room, but can meet other dogs if it feels like company.
Dogs can romp in the dunes or gambol on the beach, all under strict
supervision, of course. The hotel boasts a doggy hairdressing salon,
which also incorporates a team of canine manicurists.

    The hotel kitchen operates to the highest standards. 'We can
accommodate any dietary preferences,' says Mr Wohlfarth, the hotel
manager, 'and of course only the finest and freshest ingredients are
used.'

    It was his late mother, Margarethe Wohlfarth, widow of the
well-known Hamburg industrialist, who gave Wohlfarth the idea
of a doggy hotel. 'She made me promise, on her deathbed, not only
to look after her beloved Pekinese Henry the Fourth, but to see to the
welfare of other dogs. Our motto is 'Make your dog happy and you
save the world.'

    So far, it certainly looks as if the dog hotel is going to be a runaway
success. The thirty-three rooms are booked up for months. There is a
suite with its own butler, but that is reserved for Pekineses.

What do you make of that? My mother laughed herself silly when I read it to her. She says she can just imagine Ramona Bottle polishing the toenails of over-bred Fifis.

And by the way, she has a job. Not Bottle, my mother. She is doing the accounts for a local wine shop. The owner is just as chaotic as she is. You probably get like that if you have to spend all day tasting wine. I think she did a lot of overtime there when I was away in Majorca with my dad. She is in very good form anyway, and so am I.

What do you think of this idea? Suppose we all meet up again on Nordfall next summer? My mother says she'll come. If your mothers want to come, they can have a good time together, and if they don't behave themselves, we can threaten them with four weeks in Wohlfarth's mother – no, doggy – improvement school.

Love Emily

13 *October*

Hi everyone,

Look, this could be a lot of nonsense, but when we were shopping in Hamburg, me and Mum and Nicholas, we saw this man on the street, and I could swear it was Kruschke. OK, he wasn't quite so fat, and he was much better dressed, but I knew him by his glass eye, even though he was wearing sunglasses. When I looked back at him, he was standing there, staring at us. I got a right shock, I can tell you. My mother says I am imagining things, that Kruschke didn't look a bit like this fellow, and anyway he drowned. But Nicholas agrees with me – that it was the guy who was so mean to the toy monkey.

It doesn't really matter if Kruschke is still alive. He can't do anything to us or to our mothers now. That makes me feel good. *Really* good.

Sophie